the sweater case
fox argall mysteries
book two

Collings MacCrae

The Collings Group

Copyright © 2022 by Lisa Blanton dba The Collings Group

All rights reserved.

No part of this book may be reproduced in any form or by any electronic or mechanical means, including information storage and retrieval systems, without written permission from the author, except for the use of brief quotations in a book review.

This book was originally published on Kindle Vella.

❦ Created with Vellum

For my family, who continue to support me. For Robyn and Nora Stoy, who alpha read and inspire me. Thanks to Beth Foxcroft for the wonderful cover, and Kendra Griffin for developmental editing and more.

cast of recurring characters

Ellis 'Fox' Argall, MD, PhD, JD (Duh, Books 1-xx) – Lieutenant and detective at Palm Beach Sheriff's Violent Crimes Division. Fox is Welsh. He lives with what used to be called Asperger's, now, ASD Level 1, a level of autism characterized by a normal to higher IQ and normal to almost normal language skills, with significant challenges in social interaction and nonverbal communication, and neuro-processing differences. He's a baritone. He holds terminal degrees in molecular biology, law, and criminal justice, as well as his medical degree. Fox speaks Welsh fluently and uses other languages liberally. [Author's Note: languages are fun!]

Grace Argall, PhD (Books 1- xx) – A bioethicist and Fox's wife of almost thirty years. Grace is Fox's main 'anchor' to support his compensations. Grace is the only woman Fox has ever loved, or even dated. They met at fifteen and married at eighteen.

Marley Argall, MD (Books 1-7+) – Fox and Grace's grown daughter. She was born in the first year of her parents' marriage. Marley put herself through medical school in Books

1-2 and is practicing medicine in Books 2-3. In Book 4, she begins training to join the FBI. Marley speaks Welsh and Spanish fluently.

Theiss is Marley's daughter, with her husband Josh.

John 'Tick' Tickman (Books 1-7+) – Sergeant and detective Palm Beach Sheriff's Violent Crimes Division, Fox's partner. He holds a Master's in English Literature. Tick is African-American, and grew up in West Palm Beach, Riviera Beach, across the new bridge from Singer Island. Well, the bridge isn't new anymore. The bridge on Blue Heron Boulevard was built years ago now.

Captain Skip Harley (Books 1-7+) – head of Palm Beach Sheriff's Violent Crimes Division. Cap comes from an immigrant family, with a Scots mother and a Welsh father. He speaks both Scots Gaelic and Welsh. Fox and Skip have a complex history going back more than 20 years.

Edgar 'Roofie' Parks (Books 1-7+) – long-time friend of Fox, pastor, also serves as a major anchor for Fox. Roofie is African-American. He met Fox in Columbus, Ohio as 'Ellis' (see The Ruin of the Watcher, Book 1) and still calls him thus. Ellis was seventeen at the time, and Roofie was twenty. They have a deep and very private history.

Roofie is married to Stella, a good friend of Grace and a nurse at a local hospital where Grace also works.

Charlotte 'Charlie' Perez, MS (Books 1-7+) – (PhD candidate as of Book 4, PhD in Forensic Science Book 5 and onward) heads up Palm Beach County Sheriff Forensic Department. Charlie is a Cuban *'balasero,'* arriving in south Florida decades ago on a raft. Her husband perished on the trip.

Ezequiel 'Ez' Gaffley, MD (Books 1-7+) – Chief Medical Examiner, Palm Beach County. Ez is a second-generation Cuban American.

Stan Baskins (Books 2-7+) – FBI agent stationed out of Miami.

Natalie Forester (Books 1-6+) — Lawyer who's obsessed with Fox. She works with Homeland Security.

prologue

YOU CAN LOSE anything in a Florida swamp. Most think Florida is all sunshine and cartoon creations. It's more humid overgrowth and genuine creatures that hide in shadowy places.

one
florida swamps are for keeps

HOBE SOUND, **Florida**

The rain had poured for days.

Joe Cutchens watches water run off the border of his property on Bridge Road, flooding the weed-clogged, roadside ditch. In multiple places, the water is already rolling across the busy county road.

"Rain is always a blessing here until it's not," Everly Cutchens says. "A river runs through it, Dad."

"Damned ditch is clogged again. The whole thing is useless. Worse than useless. Dangerous," the farmer growls, wiping the rain from his face.

"I'll call in as soon as we get back to the barn." Everly squats at the fence line. "Dad, what is the red thing caught on the branch near the road?"

Joe holds the barbed wire and leans out over the ditch. "A sweater. Like, a knitted thing." Peering closer into the rushing water, he says, "Oh, Lord, this may be something."

"Tie yourself off, Dad." Everly wraps a rope around her

father and loops it on a post. "I'll throw my weight against you."

"OK, Ev, I'll go slow. Yank me up if I start to slip."

"Eyes open, Dad, might be gators in here!"

Joe slides into the muddy trough and wades through the gray-green stream. He takes multiple swipes at the red material before he's able to drag the dripping blob out. "A sweater, but no one's parts are attached."

Laughing in relief, he tosses the recovered object up to his daughter. "Floating. I dunno what I thought. Whatever. Help me back up. The side is slick and I don't want to fall back into this ditch."

Martin County Sheriff's Department

"Dammit, Howell, these ditches are a problem! I about drowned getting this thing out of the water at my northeast fence line." Joe Cutchens throws the drenched sweater material on the front desk at the Martin county sheriff's office.

"Why the hell would you do such a fool-ass thing, Joe?" Sheriff Howell Farling frowns at his old friend.

"I thought it was a kid! You think I wade in gator trenches for fun? We need something done with every ditch on Bridge Road. Overgrown with vines now and not fit for purpose."

"Leave this thing here," Howell sighs. "I'll use the mess as a prop with Geoff when the Palm Beach - Martin Sheriff's Task Force meets later today. We will try to go in sideways with Roads and describe a potential danger."

"There's a real danger, Sheriff. Would you step into one of those ditches?"

"I'm born-and-raised, like you, Joe. I wouldn't walk in a

deep puddle anywhere in Florida. Leave me the mess, let me work my magic."

The Palm Beach County Sheriff's Department, West Palm Beach, Florida

Captain Skip Harley turns his back on his lieutenant and walks to his perfectly placed orchids.

"Dammit, Fox, I assigned you to this Task Force. You do *not* choose your assignments! Be at the Martin County Sheriff's office at 1 p.m., unless you want to meet the Task Force for lunch at Harry and the Natives. Like this would ever happen. Hear me? The subject is closed. No discussion. Period."

Cap's office is a shining example of OCD, and his prized orchids are the crown jewel. If you show too much interest, the senior officer will throw Latin genera around like leaves falling in the autumn.

Detective Lieutenant Fox Argall sprawls on the chair in front of his boss's desk, playing Brick Breaker on his phone. "I'm seriously not the best choice for this. Tick, well, he's nicer than me. They will like Tick, and voila, they will like you. All of which is unlikely with me."

Cap turns to his subordinate. "Well, you're threatening me, Lieutenant Argall. Or should I say, Doctor Argall, as the entire point of you being on this task force is your fucking over-educated background. Tick is a helluva lot nicer than you, but he has no law degree or medical background in molecular genetics. People who don't know you think your brain makes you an asset, even if we understand it is a black-fucking-hole of assholishness."

"Surely not a proper word? American English is still a

mystery to me, decades on. I ask myself, is this actually English? A bit like a mixed metaphor, as well." Fox never looks up from his game.

Cap understands his lieutenant well. Too well.

Fox is a Welsh immigrant, arriving in the country at age fifteen as an exchange student in a gifted program. Multiple offers for scholarships later, he stayed, becoming a U.S. citizen in medical school while at The Ohio State University in Columbus, Ohio.

Cap's mother is Scots, but his father was also first-generation Welsh, from a town near where Fox grew up.

The two men met first in Boston, Massachusetts, when Fox was still working as an attorney for a giant law firm. Together, they took on a powerful enemy threatening Fox's family. The hell-bonding they have experienced creates an unusual working relationship.

"You will go to the Task meeting and pretend to be a normal human. *Byddwch yn* fucking normal, *am unwaith.*" Cap waves his hand at his subordinate, motioning him out.

Fox strolls from his captain's pristine glassed office into the dirt-stained Violent Crimes department as his partner, Sergeant John "Tick" Tickman, walks in. The lieutenant taps his watch and points to the wall clock. 7:05 a.m.

"Ticker, my *consigliere*, my trusted one. Once more, I have finished our morning report with the captain in your absence, consequent to your pathologic tardiness." Fox gestures to the coffee room. "We can grab coffee and discuss our afternoon meeting with the Martin - Palm Beach Task Force. You have been specially chosen to delegate our fine department. Cracking good, you."

"I'm not drinking swill. I'm also dubious of my delegation. Coulda sworn that was you, Boss."

Fox ignores Tick, but heads to the door. "Bourgeois swill it is."

Cap yells out the door. "Fox, Ticker. Head to Riviera Beach, they found a body. I'll text the address."

two
a better way to die

SINGER GARDENS, Singer Island, Riviera Beach, Florida

Two Riviera Beach police officers stand on the ninth floor of an ocean-side condo, looking down at the expensive rug and avoiding the detectives' eyes.

Tick shrugs. "Yes, the body is, in truth, a body, and the body is dead. Agreed, not in an expected place, but this alone doesn't make this situation one for Violent Crimes, Sammy."

The officers shuffle, not meeting the sergeant's gaze.

Tick smiles and pats the young man on the shoulder. "The fact we're cousins doesn't mean you should call my captain whenever you want. Captain Harley? His heart is set on my partner and me staying in our lane. Seriously, guys. This specific body is in his own home and... I dunno, 104 years old or so?"

Fox leans against the entry door frame, the catchy background beat of Brick Breaker thumping.

The second young officer frowns, looking at the doorway

toward the lieutenant. "Sergeant Tickman, this guy is kinda famous. We thought maybe Dr. Argall should check him out."

Sammy nods in agreement.

"Ah, well, 'kinda famous' is a complication. Naked on the balcony? A brain twister, for sure. But, guys. Not a case for Violent Crimes unless the Medical Examiner decides the crime is violent. You call the M.E.'s office?"

The Riviera cops glance at Fox, who pays no attention to them.

"My partner and I have an important Task Force meeting at noon. Let me call the Medical Examiner. Dr. Argall and I'll hang around if Dr. Gaffley can send someone soon."

The detective raises his eyes to his sergeant and winks.

Tick flips him off behind his back, grinning at the officers. "The examiner's office will straighten all this out."

Like magic, Chief Medical Examiner Ezekiel Gaffley appears and strolls past Fox into the condo apartment.

Tick exhales and chuckles. "See, boys? He's here to answer all the questions. You got a new psychic transport system, Doc? I mentioned you, like, two minutes ago. How did you find us so fast? We got a naked dead guy."

"Dr. Argall called me ten minutes ago. Said 'naked with bourbon.' Sounds interesting. I was driving by and thought I'd take a gander. Wassup?"

The medical examiner is an example of how to live life well. He's easy-going until you cross him, and you're on your butt. He glances around the room, gesturing at Fox, who hasn't acknowledged the chief except to move out of his way.

"You tell us what's up, Doc." Tick rolls his eyes and flicks his hand at the naked, elderly man, feet covered in bright yellow socks, sitting on a chaise on his balcony. A glass of bourbon sits on the table beside the body.

"Doctor Argall. Want to assist me? I'll make you a deputy

medical examiner. Add to your curriculum vitae." Ez walks to the balcony. "A mystery, yes? You like mysteries."

Fox audibly groans but pulls himself away from his game. "Not likely a mystery. Clear cardiac arrest. You'll find nothing to exert yourself here. This boy went out exactly as he dreamt. Bang on, I'd say. Here are the bikinis at the Hilton below, and drinking the best bourbon."

He points to the bottle of Blanton's bourbon on the floor beside the naked guy and peers theatrically over the side of the balcony toward the hotel.

"So, you just called for my company?" Ez motions for the local cops to move away, and he squats next to the body.

"Our desire for your company, certainly, plus Florida state law requiring clearance from your office for any unexplained death. The gentleman left his will over here." Fox picks up a piece of paper and reads: "'I, Reginald Carrow, wish to be buried at sea.' One choice for the death certificate. Or 'death unattended.' Your pick."

"Thanks for letting me choose."

"We can jump on the sea burial, as we're right here at the beautiful Atlantic Ocean, to fulfill his last wish."

The Riviera cops appear worried, but Ez pats Sammy as he walks around the body. "No sea burials today, my friends. I'm certain Dr. Argall is correct about the cause of death. But let's examine everything anyway, yes?"

The medical examiner motions for his photographer. "Please document the scene. Game at the Argall house Sunday, *compadre*?"

Ez Gaffley is happily married, but kind of in love with Grace Argall, Fox's wife. The relationship is entirely about food. "Grace mentioned *picadillo*. *Ropa vieja*. 'Better than *la piquera*.' Quite a claim." He finishes with the body and pulls off his gloves.

"Absolutely," Fox mumbles from the door. "You must

appear as commanded and keep my lovely wife happy, *o si no, verás*. [otherwise, you'll see]. Tick and I are off. Some naff meetings. Later, *asere*."

Ez swings his finger to the door and pats the worried beat cop on the shoulder again. "Let's move the body to my place. Death takes us all, and I'm paid to be suspicious. However, I agree with my colleague. This appears to be a marvelous way to go."

three
wildly disinterested is more like it

MARTIN COUNTY SHERIFF'S Department

"Cap is gonna be pissed." Tick walks a step in front of Fox as they arrive at the Martin County Sheriff's Department.

"Nah. Cap understands networking is not my forte. You're my subordinate, Ticker. I order you to come and be my wingman. In fact, my frontman. Thus, you're off the hook."

"I'm your freaking babysitter, Shay," Tick laughs. "I'm never off the hook."

Tick often calls Fox 'Shay,' which is short for Seamus, an Irish name. The first time he called Fox 'Seamus,' he had timed the jibe perfectly for a rare Fox conniption. His Welshman partner went on forever about where Ireland was, and how Ireland isn't Wales, and something derogatory about American ignorance. Still made him laugh. "Cap might hit me if I used 'he ordered me' as an excuse."

"Well." Fox's go-to phrase when he's irritated or simply done talking. He's rarely irritated and often done talking.

Shoving Fox, Tick says, "Ah, what the hell-o, I'll back your play at these meetings. I got nothing better. Unless Cap calls.

The Sweater Case

He calls, and I'm absolutely making background noises like I'm in the loo at the station. Swoosh, right?"

"Lovely job on not cursing and crikey, using 'loo,' bravo," Fox laughs. "Better job on 'backing my play.' You won't regret the stand."

Tick groans. "Sounds like a foreshadow in a mystery thriller. The ones that never end well?"

Pulling open the door into the Martin County Sheriff's office, Tick heads to the desk. "Hey, man, where do we go for the county Task Force meeting?"

The desk officer points behind them at the door. "They are coming in behind you from lunch, now."

The door slides open, Florida heat pushing in. A group of five men and a woman fill the small entry.

Tick thrusts his hand out to the nearest person, the woman. "I'm Sergeant John Tickman from Violent Crimes out of Palm Beach. We're here for the Task Force."

"I'm Deputy Ann Carley, Martin County. This is our team. Are you the full crew from PB?"

Tick turns to find Fox, who is nowhere to be found. "Uh, Lieutenant Argall was here a minute ago."

"I think he's down here," the desk clerk answers nervously. "Are you Lieutenant Argall, uh... Sir?"

Fox is squatting on the floor behind the front desk, staring intently at a piece of fabric in a wire cabinet. "Where did this material come from?"

Howell Farling, the sheriff for Martin county, walks over and peers down at the detective. "Just came in this morning from a farmer. Farm off Bridge Road. He found the material in a run-off ditch."

"Where on Bridge Road?" Fox stands up. "Where is the farm located?"

"His property runs to Hobe Sound, bounded by Jonathan Dickinson State Park, and I95. He's got some land over across the interstate, but they found this nearer to Hobe Sound. Mind sharing your thoughts? I assume you're Dr. Argall?" Howell waves his hand to the group.

The detective startles, noticing the gathering for the first time. "Fox. I'm Fox, of course," he says, missing the cue to explain his focus on the red material.

Tick sighs. "I'm Lieutenant Argall's social director. Yes, this is Dr. Ellis Argall. He goes by 'Fox' to most people. We will take this interaction as a harmless warning. Dr. Argall will go off on tangents and struggle to care about what a lot of other people might think of as important. Like Task Force meetings."

"Crikey, Ticker. Harsh. I'm not even on Brick Breaker." Fox pushes his Welsh accent and throws a dazzling smile at the group. The group visibly relaxes, and Howell smiles.

"Oh, for fuck's sake," Tick mumbles.

Fox glances at his partner, but says, "Of course, I'm assigned to this Task Force in part because I have academic backgrounds in medicine and law."

"Dr. Argall is being humble." Howell Farling starts.

"Freaking unlikely," Tick interrupts. "He's too focused on the red thing to bother."

"Well, Ticker," Fox says, "you have a point. An important point. Here's the real question. Do you have a pair of gloves and a bag sized for this? This is evidence." He points at the material, looking at his partner.

Sheriff Farling motions to the desk clerk, but Ann Carley leans over and hands Fox the gloves and bag.

"Dr. Argall, can you explain your thinking to us?" Ann says.

"This is a piece of a sweater. I think a woman's, but now children are dressed more maturely..." Fox frowns. "Well, possibly a child's."

He takes too long with the gloves, messing with the

fingers. Finally, he gives up, smiling at the group watching him. Folding a glove in half, he protects two fingers to put the material in the bag.

He lifts the material to the light, moving the yarn around inside the bag. "A wide weave with a large yarn width, yes? This section is red, but with a lot of white strings... also yarn? We don't know yet. Right here? This is blood. Human? Maybe. Yet, here is our problem. This brown stain? I think we have liquid methamphetamine. An unusual odor. Kinda like fingernail polish mixed with feline urine."

Howell works hard to stop from rolling his eyes. "The thing was floating in a ditch of run-off water. Meth is highly soluble. The yarn is red, for God's sake. How are you so sure about the blood?"

"The blood is actually coffee-ground consistency mixed with other vomitus. Right here?" Fox points to a small clump of something dark hidden in the broad weave. "Might be wrong, of course. Better safe. I suspect this material floated quite readily, and the open weave of water-resistant yarn may have helped us here. We will find out. Let's consider forensics."

Ann motions the group into a room down the hall. "As everyone describes, Dr. Argall is wildly over-educated. A PhD in Molecular Genetics, an active Medical Degree, and an active -- meaning he can practice here -- law license. We shouldn't neglect the bonus PhD in criminology, should we?" Ann guides Fox to a chair, but she smiles at Tick. The smile doesn't make her brown eyes.

Tick groans. *Jealousy, shit, all we need is someone who thinks they need to compete with Fox.* This macho reaction is normal in some men, but he can't remember envy in a woman.

Women all swoon at his partner. Tick is forced to admit Fox is what anyone would call handsome. He turns on his charm and accent and usually stops — or starts — all kinds of problems.

"Hey, guys," Tick says. "We're never sure when my partner is right, but we accept mostly always. At Palm Beach, we've just learned to roll with him. Now. Do we talk about what the new evidence might mean, or should we put the sweater case on the shelf and start Task Force stuff?"

Tick always takes charge of interactions. Except with Cap, who has known Fox for decades. Tick tries to hide when those two scuffle, which is too often for Tick's post-traumatic hyper-vigilance. *Cap is gonna be so pissed.*

Howell moves to the whiteboard. "Let's start the Task Force meeting and send this to forensics. No need to chew on unknowns."

Fox is playing Brick Breaker and doesn't look up. "Let's bring Charlie in, Tick. She's the best. County politics aren't a problem, Martin sends their forensics out to Palm Beach. No toes cramped."

"We can hear you." Howell grins. The Sheriff appears genuinely friendly.

Smiling vaguely, Fox doesn't respond. He has no idea who's talking.

Tick finds no malice in Sheriff Howell. Ann Carley is a different story.

four
threads of evidence begin to unravel

TICK'S *voice booms out of the darkness. "Coming from the corner! Incoming!"*

The dark shape slams into me so fast I'm unable to move or defend myself. My head whips back, crashing on the concrete as legs wrap around me like a TV wrestler. A Max-9 Ruger is pointed right at my face. Wait, a Max-9? A micro? A woman's...?

Fox startles awake, struggling to lift a sudden weight.

"Hullo, husband." Grace straddles him, her nose touching his. Her elbows press into his chest.

"Hullo, wife. You want something? I was sleeping."

"You were rolling."

"Yes. Well. You need something?"

"I do."

"Something I can help you with?"

"I'm not sure. Possibly."

"Ah. 'Possibly.' You should be more specific, Gracie. Your elbows are weapons, and I'm in pain here."

"Here is my weapon, husband." She holds up a pink sparkly bottle of Pharma Magic Elixir.

He squints at his wife. "My magic lotion, stolen from my nightstand. And you're wondering if I can help? I assure you, I can." In a fast flip, he pins her on the king-sized bed. "I have several effective weapons."

"Naaahh! Nan! Na Nah!" A tiny voice floats under their door.

Fox moans, throwing himself sideways. "Go, go. Good grief, Leona."

"Coming, Theissey!" Grace narrows her eyes. "Who is this Leona you've brought into our bed?"

The phone rings on Fox's nightstand. *Cap's ring.* The time glows green. *Four a.m.*

"Wife! Four a.m.?" But she's in the hall, turning into their granddaughter's room.

"Argall. The time is four a.m.," the detective growls into the phone.

"Lieutenant Argall." Cap barks. "The bloody half-a sweater you found on the front desk at Martin county sheriff? The one the farmer brought in? Blood's human. And we found what appears to be the other half of the sweater, hanging off the top rails of the Jupiter Lighthouse. Seven miles away from the original scene and 100 feet up. The property was closed. You're on deck, Doc. Meet your boy Tick at the Inlet Light ASAP. My guys tell me you're fifteen away."

"'Fifteen away'? Your guys? You have those kinds of guys now?" The call disconnects.

Falling backward on the bed, he yells to Grace. "That was Cap. I'm sent out."

"Shhh!"

"Good grief, Leona."

The Sweater Case

"I'm not going up." Tick won't even glance at the Lighthouse.

The Inlet Light sits on the north side of the stunning estuary where the Atlantic Ocean flows into the Loxahatchee River between Jupiter and Tequesta.

Fox stares up at the bright red conical structure. "The tower is 105 feet tall and 153 feet above sea level. First lit in 1860. Most of the German U-boats discovered and destroyed in WWII were located by this station."

"Yay. I'm still not going up this skinny death trap."

"Ticker. This is new. You're afraid of heights? You were a paratrooper. A Ranger. Appears incongruent."

"Not exactly. In the air, I'm in control of the plane or I strap a chute on my back. Not climbing a 200-year-old upside-down ice cream cone. I don't fit. I refuse to climb up those freaking stacked mini-shelves they call stairs."

"Just over 150 years old, actually. Your math is bad, but your point is taken. I need to examine the evidence in its original setting, anyway. Think of how lovely the sunrise will be from here." The detective tilts his head at the Jupiter cop standing outside the entry door. "No one has trudged up and down?"

"Nah, Lieutenant."

"I have to ask. *Mynd o flaen gofid*. Assume the worst."

"No one up there but me, Dr. Argall. A homeowner over in the Inlet Colony was looking 'at stars,'" the stocky, middle-aged officer says with air quotes, "and called about this material on the railing. I went up alone. Gloves and booties. I was concerned because the Lighthouse is closed."

Fox salutes the cop. "Come, Ticker."

"I'm not going in. I'll be in the car. *Not* going in. Assume the worst is right."

"The saying translates more like 'we'll cross the bridge if we have to.' Try to remain positive." The detective's voice echoes as he starts up the inside stairs of the narrow structure.

"Wait!" Tick yells into the tower.

"What?"

"Do you have booties? The correct size gloves and an evidence bag? No, you do not. Come take these. Damn, Shay. You're supposed to be the freaking scientist."

Fox snatches the protective gear and heads back up.

Ten minutes later, he leans over the top railing. "Tick, I think you need to examine this."

"Bring whatever down."

"No, I mean, examine *in situ*, assess the evidence in place, as originally located."

"I know what *in situ* means, dammit. I'll call Charlie."

"No, this is a Tick thing. Sorry, pet. I am."

"Fucking damn. Damn-nation. Don't call me freaking pet," Tick growls, punching the car seat.

"I can't hear you."

Stalking to the tower, he thrusts his head through the tiny door to the Lighthouse and yells up the swirling steps. "I said FUCK!"

Fifteen minutes later, the big sergeant appears on the top balcony. "I'm serious. This better be needful."

"Needful?" Fox snorts. "Are you quoting from some woman's magazine you read last night? And they say *I'm* odd."

"You *are* odd, Shay. Now, what do you need from me? I'm here."

"Come. Observe and describe the scene." The detective points his phone light at a piece of red yarn hanging off the top rail.

A copper penny odor wafts in the breeze coming off the ocean as it rushes into the Jupiter Inlet. Blood drips on the concrete floor of the balcony surrounding the top of the Lighthouse.

The Sweater Case

"The fabric is soaked with fresh blood. A lot of blood." Tick flexes his jaw. "Like, a lot."

"Anything else?"

Tick leans in with his own light, grimacing. "Material is the same stuff from the Martin county sheriff's and... oh, man. Dammit, a lip. Ah, hell, Shay, you're the physician, but it looks like a human lip."

"A lip. Cracking job, you. A top lip, in fact. But I'm talking about this fabric here." Fox points to another textile, thin and coarse, underneath the woven sweater. The strip of multiple colors is at the top of the metal rail, almost hidden.

"Well, hard to tell, especially in this light. A ribbon. You said the yarn might be from a kid's sweater. Don't they have decorations sometimes?"

"Is it military?"

Tick peers closer, leaning over the edge. "Shit. Yes, could be. I think so. An Army combat award."

"Well, Bob's your uncle. This is a quick little win." Fox claps his hands.

"Ah. The elusive Argall grin." Tick flares. "Like a real, human-being smile. Glee, as I fall for your stunt to drag me up here?"

The older man's face falls. "Why, really? Yesterday, you were mean to me at the Martin county meeting. Now, this? What have I ever done?"

"Aww..." Tick groans with sudden remorse.

"Of course, it's not a stunt. Have you met me? Am I capable of such an elaborate joke? I live in the moment, my friend. My best quality. Something you should try."

"'Living in the moment.' Is that what you call what you do?"

The sunrise floods the sky with pink, golden-lined clouds sending sherbet-orange threads across the horizon.

"Red sky in the morning," Tick murmurs. "A warning. I

hate this case already, and it hasn't been three hours since you woke me."

"Told you it'd be lovely. Your poetic heart darkens even this unmatched view." Fox crouches below the hidden ribbon, peering up at the railing. "Now, here, this striated material is heavily textured. I'm betting, praying, somewhere along the line, our Sweater Handler touched this. We'll ask Charlie in forensics, but I think we have a better chance with the ribbon than the yarn base."

"Why? This yarn has been through the wringer. Wouldn't more activity against the source add to the potential for touch DNA?"

"Yes. But also, possibly no." Fox leans further toward the railing without touching anything. "'Activity,' as you refer, connotes what forensics call 'handling time,' or the time a source may touch whatever is being examined as evidence. Forensic studies tell us 'time in hand' is not the most important variable. The priority element is the skin condition of the one who leaves the deposit or 'shed.' The grooves in the ribbon are better to slough keratinized cells and — if we're lucky, perspiration, sort of floating DNA fragments. The shed is more likely scraped off on the rougher surface. More than the yarn, right? But what do I know?"

"I'd take the bet."

"I love this stuff. Like a treasure hunt." Fox stands up, his green eyes sparkling.

"Or a walk down a dark and stormy path at night in a very deserted wood."

"Well, I'm a self-selected science buff, and you're an English Literature major who happens to be a cop."

"There's that."

five
in the frame

PALM BEACH COUNTY Sheriff's Complex, Forensics Department

The Palm Beach County Crime Labs are housed in the main detention center at the sheriff's headquarters, in the same concrete complex as Violent Crimes.

"You're a lucky lady, Charlie." Fox wanders around the bright, white laboratory. "New labs. Plenty of windows for natural light. Look at the room! You come to work, you do anything you want. A matrix-assisted laser desorption ionization time-of-flight mass spectrometer. Like eternal Christmas."

"We have blood on the original piece of sweater you sent in, Dr. Fox, and *el vómito*, as you suspected." Charlotte 'Charlie' Perez taps her computer screen. "Print out?"

"Not much for paper. What's on your wish list? Want me to make sure you spend your budget wisely?"

"More equipment, more data for you to smush through, doctor." She hands him a folded sheet, pointing to a pink highlighted area. "I've got a minor complication for you."

"Ah, pet. You always give gold." Fox takes the report, eyes twinkling. "This place makes me happy, and you're one of my favorites. Catch me up."

"The coffee-ground blood is female, as is the vomitus. The biologic profile *es bueno* and we ran the specimen. No hit. *Nada. Interesante.* The weave is not American. The textile was woven in Mexico. *Especifico*, from a small town in the central portion called Chapultepec, outside Toluca. No *producido en masa*, no. Hand-loomed and dyed."

"Quite the level of detail."

"The looming is much looser than anything mass-produced. Made for a colder climate, like some mountainous areas around Mexico City." Charlie pulls a colorful vest off her desk. "This lovely garment was sent to a friend from an *artiste* near Toluca. Examine this as a sample. We're adding some tests to determine how similar."

"Mountainous Mexico or the climes of the northern states of the U.S., like Detroit." Fox wrinkles his nose in thought. "I'm concerned about the brown stain. Liquid meth?"

"Ah, *si*. Lower quality. Possibly for transportation, to augment later."

"Can you tell if the meth spilled first, before the blood?"

"*Si*, in several spots. Blood lies on top of the meth-amphetamine under what appears to be a sleeve. Difficult to know the original shape, given the unwinding of the yarns." Charlie holds the weave up to the light. "Here is one spot, yes?"

"Yes. This leaves us with some data points. The drug stain occurred, and then significant bleeding on the fabric. What am I missing?"

Charlie frowns and hands him another report. "High levels of troponin in the blood found at the scene. Super high levels. It's possible the donor received CPR for an extended period."

"CPR. To be accurate, without a complete body, the lip came from a body with probable death. This assumes we'll have a body for the lip. Why perform CPR if you intended to murder? The amount of blood at the scene may indicate severe injury incidental to another ongoing crime."

"So victim in the proverbial wrong place."

"Or a purposeful assault and someone present didn't agree with the decisions." Fox's dark brows draw down. "Tried to stop the death for some reason."

"If the reason matters," she shrugs. "A collection of ideas about this death is forming, but we're missing critical information."

"OK. The troponin level is important. Another data point. What about the military award?"

The forensic scientist turns away from the detective to a lab table. "The ribbon. I have nothing back yet. I'll text you asap."

"Charlie," Fox murmurs. "What are you hiding from me?"

"Hiding? *No seas fresco.*"

"Ah, 'don't get fresh.' Hmm. Your misdirection is not even sufficient to misdirect me. Tell me what worries you."

She walks across her lab before turning. "Lieutenant. The tests are not complete. Jumping to conclusions, *que pesa'o.*" [much drama.]

"You have clearly already jumped, my friend. Why don't you let me share your burden? I'm fundamentally incapable of the *pesa'o* to which you refer."

Balling her fists, Charlie inhales. "The ribbon. There's a lot of cutaneous material, mostly anucleated, and saliva. The profile is clear, and we have it on record. The DNA belongs to John Tickman."

six
detested chaises and dumped bodies

GRACE PULLS INTO THE GARAGE. The house is dark, as usual. Fox is rarely home before her.

I better set the alarm. Avoid a lecture from my husband. She lowers her backpack into the rack by the kitchen door and moves wearily to the stairs.

"Gracie."

She drops her purse, scattering contents everywhere.

"Fox? You scared me!"

He's stretched out on the flowered chaise he hates. The day she had it delivered, he threw a tiny fit. *What is this odd couch thing? Who are we? Royalty?* He repeats the complaint almost every day. She isn't sure if it's a campaign to break her down or if her husband's compulsive brain views the furniture as a new irritation each time.

"Fox? Are you OK, honey?"

"No. I'm not OK." His voice is tight. "Nothing is OK."

"Ellis Argall, explain. You're scaring me."

"Ah, our kids are fine," he groans. "No one we know is dead or injured. I apologize for the incomplete whinge."

"Better complete it, sweet Ladislaw." She climbs onto the

chaise, folding herself behind her husband. "Tell me what bothers you."

"There's a problem. One I can't figure how to solve."

"Are you supposed to fix it?"

He pulls into a fetal position, silent.

"Honey, is it your responsibility to fix something? Describe what happened. Tell me all of it." She loosens her husband's tie and removes his shoes. "You hate this couch, but the house rule about shoes on the furniture is still in play."

"Want a Red Hot?" He strokes her face, rolling on top of her. "I think I've discovered what you see in this hideous couch."

Hours are long and late for homicide detectives. The danger and fear are too real, and time is precious. Decades ago, the Argalls agreed to keep Red Hots candy on their nightstands. 'Any Time' is their promise to each other. Fox needs his connection to Grace to survive.

"Always, dear Lad. Does this replace explaining your problem or just delay it?"

He doesn't answer. He covers his wife's mouth with his and pulls her hands to his hips.

Grace waits for Fox's steady breathing before she gets up from the chaise. As she moves, the front door opens, and their daughter Marley steps in.

"Moms! Moms, where are you? Upstairs? Kitchen?"

"Lad, wake up, honey. Cover yourself." She shoves him off the couch and grabs one of the dozen soft blankets strewn across her home and throws it over her naked husband.

"What?" Fox grumbles, sitting up.

"Wait! Marley, give me a minute, wait." She draws a

second throw around her like a towel. "Do not turn on the light."

Marley pretends to cover her eyes, giggling. "Eww, you guys! What if I had Josh and Theiss with me? No worries, though. I'm a trained physician. You have nothing I've not seen several times." She drops on the stairs, head in her lap.

Fox wraps the blanket at his waist, gathering his clothes as he walks to the master bedroom. "I object to being shoved onto the floor."

"Ellis Argall. Quiet." Grace points at her daughter. "You should *knock*."

"Moms. It's like... not even 7 p.m. When would Dad ever be home this early?" Marley can't stop laughing. "Besides, it's not like I don't have a lot of experience with you two. You've always been like rabbits. Bunnies going at it."

"*Marley Argall*. Stop this instant. You're being disrespectful." Grace's face is blazing, a bonus she gets with her red, curly hair. "I'm always glad to see you, but is everything OK? Aren't you on call?"

"Yes, Moms, but I've got a strange incident I need to tell you about. I was going to ask you before saying anything to Dad, but seeing as he's here."

Fox comes to the living room, dressed in sweatpants and a tee shirt. He leans against the door frame. "Strange incident?"

"Dad, sit down, would you? Can you guys sit down?"

Marley's green eyes echo her father's. *Those eyes look inside and capture you somehow.*

"I don't think so." The detective spins his phone in his hand. "I think I'm bang on right here." He begins to play with his phone, running away to Brick Breaker, his video hiding place.

"Daddy, *os gwelwch yn dda. I fi*. Please. For me."

He edges over to a chair close to the door and perches on the arm.

"OK, if that's all you'll give me. I'm working the ER today and a body came in. A female, in her late teens or early twenties. Tossed out of a van at the emergency door. Partially clothed. Her chest was so contused, the injury confused me at first. Broken sternum. I mean, broken into two pieces. No sexual assault. Here's the weird thing. The injuries to her chest? I'm certain they're from a CPR attempt."

"Her lip?" He murmurs, not looking up.

"Her upper lip was roughly excised. No technique, mind you, but purposeful, with a sharp knife. How did you know?" Marley flicks a glance at her mother.

"You drove 75 miles from Miami in the rush-hour insanity of Interstate 95 to talk to your mother in person. Your mother. Not your father, the police detective who is a physician. Yet, we learn about dumped bodies and excised lips. Why?" He's staring at his phone, but his thumbs aren't moving.

Grace walks to her daughter, standing between her child and her husband. "Ellis. If Marley felt it best to..."

He puts his phone on the end table. "Let's just deal with this, girlie."

Marley's jaw clenches as she faces her father, pink spots rising on her cheeks. "The woman had Tick's driver's license in her back pocket. It isn't current, it's an older one, but it's Tick, John Tickman."

"Did you call this in?" Fox stands up and locks eyes with his daughter.

His mini-me. How they mirror each other. Mounds of curly, dark hair, and light green feline eyes. The familiar, graceful stance. They're two sides of the same coin.

"Not yet." Marley doesn't break her father's gaze.

"Well. Let's hold off on that."

"I can get another hour. Afterward, I go off call and have to transfer the case."

"Give me as much time as you can." He wriggles into his shoulder holster and squats to his gun safe below the table. "I've got to think. No idea when I'll be back, Gracie."

Marley slips her arm to Grace's waist as they watch him adjust an ankle holster.

He never wears an ankle holster.

seven
familiarity and other harmful things

"WE'RE DRIVING TO MIAMI?" Tick sits in the passenger seat of Fox's personal car, back straight and voice strained. "It's 8:30 p.m."

"I'm driving to Miami. I have no idea where you are."

"Man, give me more to work with here. You're creeping me out. Do you need fresh blue crab? A real Cuban sandwich? A therapeutic blood level of some medication?"

"I'm going to Jackson Memorial to meet an old friend who is chief of staff. A body was dumped at the door of the Emergency Department. It may be connected to our Sweater Case. Nothing more right now."

The SUV's motor is whining in the workout, going 90 m.p.h. in the express lane, surrounded on every side by other cars and semi-trucks going as fast or faster.

"Nothing more?" Tick tightens and braces his feet against the floor. "You're flying."

"This is Interstate 95 between Fort Lauderdale and Miami. Remember what you told me the first time you drove me down? Buckle in if you're a newbie."

"OK, man, but you don't drive a bunch, and you're legit

scaring me. Give me something. Is Cap going to blow on this?"

"Your dubious tone insults me. Driving is not my favorite thing — but, no offense, you Floridians are nuts. As for Cap, this is our case. Who else would go inspect a body connected to our work?"

"OK. You're projecting massive anxiety, Lieutenant. You planning on explaining?"

"No."

Frank Matthews reaches out to shake hands. "They dumped the body in front of the Emergency Department. I think Marley was working the ER at the time. Can I assume she called you?"

"You can assume that." Fox drops back to avoid the welcome gesture and flicks his hand at Tick. "This is my sergeant. We may have the excised upper lip. Found in a scene on top of the Jupiter Inlet Light."

"On top of the tower? Whoa. OK. Didn't read this bit in the news. Are you going to move the body to Ez?" Frank narrows his eyes at his friend. "You're skittery. Something more than a dumped Jane Doe worrying you?"

Ez Gaffley, Frank Matthews, and Fox are on the board of a medical charity. They volunteer to provide care to those unable to pay, running a family health group in West Palm.

Fox stiffens and flips his phone between his hands. "I'm involving Ez's office. May I examine the body?"

"We had to cool the body down, so we moved it. We work to maintain a limited chain of custody. Our procedures don't always align perfectly with yours. Not as rare as we'd like to have a body dumped."

"Understood, Dr. Matthews." The detective waves the

group to the door, impatient. "We need to alter procedures to include an immediate call to Violent Crimes if an assault is suspected."

Frank punches his speakerphone. "Liz, is Marley Argall gone? No matter, page her, please. Tell her to meet me and her father at the morgue."

As they leave the room, Fox puts his hand on Tick's shoulder. "Sergeant, can you keep the hallway clear outside the morgue? We need some privacy. If Marley shows, just send her in directly."

Tick shudders under his touch.

The morgue is deep in the basement, cool and shadowed, even quieter this time of night. Marley is leaning on the gray-green wall by the elevator as the group exits.

"My sergeant is going to keep the hall open while we examine the body." Fox leads them to the morgue's double metal doors. He doesn't look at his daughter. "Marley, please accompany Dr. Matthews and me and give us your report on the situation."

Marley's face is aflame with embarrassment and concern. Tick is pale and silent, moving back against the wall.

A cool breeze swooshes over the group as they enter the morgue. The tech, Leanne, is waiting for them, the body pulled out and on a metal table and covered with a hospital green sheet.

"Leanne, can you follow up and verify Dr. Gaffley is properly notified?" Frank Matthews pulls the sheet down from the damaged face.

A hot flash of panic bursts in Fox's chest. He shivers to collect himself, glancing up into his daughter's gaze. "Well. We'll need to call my captain, Skip Harley. Frank, you met Skip? While the facial injuries complicate matters, I believe this is a young lady familiar to me."

It's Tick's recent girlfriend. It's Dalia.

eight
orchids don't smell but that's not all

CAPTAIN SKIP HARLEY leans against his custom-built orchid display, head in his precious flowers. "So, we have a problem."

"We do." Fox stands at the window, flipping his phone in his hand. "You realize those orchids of yours are multiplying, spreading out. Kinda like a cancer. You're going to need gardeners from the property here to manage them."

"A beautiful cancer." Cap smiles. "Let's concentrate here. Give me the complete picture laid out so I can decide how to proceed. We don't want to risk Tick by either including him or excluding him inappropriately. *Helpwch fi. Gosodwch y cyfan allan.*" [Help me. Lay it all out.]

"Here's the evidence to date. I found a piece of fabric, yarn-like, at the Martin county sheriff's, during the Task Force meeting. I thought the material had coffee-ground blood in the weave, and an odor of methamphetamine from a stain. Forensics later confirmed both thoughts. You've seen the report?" His voice fades as he stares out the window, the Brick Breaker tune playing in the background.

"Yes. I'll go to Charlie to review everything. I'd like you to come with me. Finish the summary."

"Tick and I were in Stuart for the Task Force. He was present when I examined the material at the Martin county meeting. It appeared to be a part of a sweater. Within 48 hours, Jupiter Inlet Police found a torn garment very similar to the woven fabric on the Inlet Light. Tick went with me to the scene. Charlie agrees the two pieces are from the same main; clothing for an older child or small adult, made in Mexico. With me so far?"

Cap rolls his eyes. "Think I can follow, dunce that I am. Continue."

"The Lighthouse scene was quite gory. The material was soaked, and blood dripped onto the concrete floor below. A roughly excised upper lip was lashed through the yarn. The amount of blood loss we would expect from the lip wouldn't have accounted for the amount on the balcony. Subsequently, Charlie found the lip was removed after death occurred, further proof the blood wasn't from the lip. You told me orchids don't have a fragrance. Why do you like them? I've never asked."

Cap laughs. "You wouldn't be asking now if you weren't freaking out about our Tick problem."

"I never 'freak out.' I do like orchids. They're oddly plastic-looking."

"A weirdo reason to like a flower. Let's focus on the case. Afterward, I'll buy you a drink and tell you all about my love of orchids."

Fox exhales and slings himself into a tufted chair across from Cap's giant, pristine desk. "Hiyo. Peri-mortem lip excision. Another piece of material, in addition to the sweater at the Lighthouse scene. A ribbon. A military award ribbon. Army combat. While we have confirmed nothing of provenance, it's Tick's DNA."

"A key point and a missed entry into your report on the scene."

"Yes, well." Brick Breaker on, the detective doesn't look up.

"*Rydw i ar eich ochr chi*. I'm on your side. On Tick's side, unless proven impossible." Cap sits in the matching chair next to his subordinate. "I'm asking nicely, Dr. Argall. Don't shut me out. As much as you find this difficult, I'm an asset. An asset you can't match. I'll pull rank if necessary."

"The situation has passed my control. I acquiesce; I need you. Blood belonging to the dumped body is also on the ribbon, albeit on top of Tick's DNA. Mixed with other DNA, as yet unknown. Of course, we would expect multiple profiles on a combat ribbon. The blood at the Lighthouse and the morgue body match. Charlie also found high levels of troponin — a cardiac enzyme — in the victim's blood. Troponin can indicate attempted CPR, among other possibilities."

"Any additional evidence?" The senior officer shrugs. "Troponin isn't common, but not unheard of in homicides. Why is troponin important? Doesn't the same stuff show up in heart attacks? "

"Maybe. Possibly." Fox shakes his head. "Not at these levels. Way too high. The woman dumped at Jackson was severely contused in her chest area. Marley was the physician on duty at the time. She told me the damage appeared to be from CPR attempts, without any knowledge of the lab results. The sternum was broken. I've tentatively identified the body as Dalia Roberts, RN. She works, er, worked at Jupiter Medical Center. She's been on a few outings with Tick. Grace and I took them to church once. We both had social interaction with the victim. Probable victim."

"OK. So, the troponin evidence from the Lighthouse scene aligns with the Jackson body. Talk to me about the possible CPR attempt."

"I dunno." Fox slurs and drops his head to his knees. "It

feels important. In a scenario, it may indicate an accidental death, or at least suggest one person present didn't agree with the killing."

"Another person, like a six-foot-six-inch cop? One familiar with the victim, knows CPR, and is strong enough to crack a chest? You assessing the possibility your partner is connected, *hen ffrind* [old friend]?"

Fox swallows and blinks.

"It's not where my head is," Cap says. "I know my team. Tick is not in this. I'll wager you a bottle of Blanton's bourbon. Not my sergeant. However, it's clear Ticker must be off the case."

"Of course. I'm fine on my own. I'll go see Charlie. Need to verify the identity of the body. Can't locate any relatives. None on the employment record at the hospital, assuming this is Dalia."

Cap straightens a stack of perfectly straight papers on his desk. "Sheriff Howell Farling would like to stay involved in the case."

"Stay involved in the case?" The detective narrows his eyes at his captain. "What does that mean?"

"Just settle down. He's already involved. You involved him."

"I did. Now I'm un-involving him." He opens the door to walk out.

Ann Carley is sitting on one of the waiting area chairs.

"Lieutenant Argall, do you remember Deputy Carley?" Cap comes up behind Fox. "She works for Howell in Martin county. The Martin team would like an update on the sweater case. We calling this one The Sweater Case? Seems appropriate."

nine
timing isn't everything

ANN CARLEY STANDS up from the chair as the men open the door. Cap nods and disappears into his office.

"Update, Lieutenant Argall?"

"Captain Harley has all the info I have." His head is in his phone game.

"Somehow, I doubt it." Carley examines the detective, arms crossed over her uniform.

"He'll be glad to update you, or your sheriff. Here's a bonus. Cap can tell you all about orchids. I'm late for a meeting." Fox glances at the deputy, cocks his head to the side, and smiles.

"The flirting works for you most of the time, doesn't it, Dr. Argall? The charm offensive? I'm afraid I'm immune."

Fox blinks, twirling his phone. Finally, he drops his head. "You're upset. The orchid comment? I'm sorry, I didn't mention orchids because you're female. Captain Harley breeds beautiful orchids — not sure of the accurate term? I'm straight biology and almost no botany."

"Botany?" Carley sneers.

"Captain Harley is thoroughly competent to explain the

science. Lovely, in a plasticky kind of way." The detective glances into his supervisor's glassed office for help.

Cap recognizes the telltale squirm and walks out. "How are you coming with your update?"

"I stepped in it, I'm afraid." Fox presses his lips together and shuffles his feet. "Suggested you were best to update Deputy Carley and recommended your orchids. Crikey, it sounds bad to me, now I consider. I meant nothing more than to suggest they were interesting. My decided lack of talent at small talk."

"Decided lack. We're aligned on one subject, at least," Cap grins at Deputy Carley. "Has my detective stepped in it? May I call you Ann?"

"Gentlemen, I don't care who updates me, to be honest. Howell would like a status report on the evidence brought into our office. I think we can agree we found the initial crime scene in Martin County."

Before Cap can answer, Fox interjects, "But we can't. I don't agree. We haven't identified the original crime scene. The Palm Beach forensics team didn't find any data pointing to the location of the assault. Not yet."

"A local farmer brought in the piece of sweater found in Martin county a day before the Lighthouse material was discovered."

Fox stares at the deputy. "The Lighthouse was closed. They could have left the evidence at any point in a range of days. We're uncertain of the timing. I have a meeting. You two must crack on without me."

Cap motions the deputy into his office. "Why don't you come in, and I'll update you. I haven't completed my review, but we can walk through it together. I do breed gorgeous orchids."

Ann Carley follows the captain in, closing the door. Fox texts his boss:

> Ask her to speak her thoughts on the timing of the crime. As much detail as you can. Write down what she says to you.

ten
forthright irony if nothing else

TICK AND FOX sit in a slippery oak pew at the back of the sanctuary in Roofie's church, waiting for the pastor to come out of a meeting.

"You're crouching so tight you're almost balled up," Fox grumbles, flipping his phone from one hand to the other. He stands and begins to pace down the aisle.

"It's like I'm in sixth grade again, and called to the principal. Why are we here?"

Fox stops and stares at his feet. "You got called to the principal's office? Did boys beat you up, too?"

"Shay, man." Tick snorts, shaking his head. "No, boys did not beat me up. I hit six feet tall the summer I had my twelfth birthday."

"I was unsure of how American schools worked for guys who liked English Literature and poetry."

"Happen often? The beatings?"

"My appearance, my... This." He stops and inhales, gesturing to his face. "The adjective used was 'pretty,' and not in a complimentary way. Well, add thinking like me, and you receive the wrong kind of attention in P-level years. My dad said I attracted violence like a magnet attracts metal."

"Aw, Shay."

"It's how I learned to fight." Fox paces again. "Actually, my sister Isla taught me. No, not taught me. I stood aside, and she beat people who wanted to beat me. I researched boxing and various martial arts."

Damn. Explains a lot. "I'd expect nothing less than a written dissertation on personal protection. Isla, huh? I want to meet her someday."

"She comes every few years. She's an athro... Don. History professor. I don't always follow how people react. I think, erroneously, people think like me, except of course they don't." His mouth draws into a thin line, eyes far away.

"How many siblings? Are they here? In the U.S.?"

"Six much older sisters. Isla is the youngest of the crew. I'm four years younger. She was my protector. They're in Wales and England. Married off before I came here permanently at sixteen to attend Ohio State."

"Sixteen." *He was a kid, dropped in a different country alone.*

"Old home week, gentlemen?" Roofie's booming voice echoes in the chancel.

The pastor hugs Fox for a long time.

He must be twitching inside being touched. Such an odd connection between these two.

"Let's go to my office unless you'd rather talk here. Or, hey! Should we worship for a while before we talk?" Roofie grins at his old friend. "It's been weeks since you've been in my pews."

Fox's jaw flexes and his eyebrows turn down.

It's strange for him to be... Compliant?

"OK, I'll leave you alone. Happy to meet you again, Tick. How're you doing?"

I have no idea how I'm doing. "Uh, OK."

"I think worship is what you two need, but let's head in.

Follow me. Anyone want coffee? We bought a real coffee maker."

"I'll always take some," Fox murmurs, hands in his pockets. "Ticker is more discerning and may reject you."

"Well, let's find out. Follow me, boys. My room is more private."

Shelves of books and stacks of song booklets fill Roofie's office. Sheets of handwritten music cover the battered oak desk, colored pens scattered across the papers. Four guitars line up behind his worn, padded desk chair.

"Jacob?" Roofie calls to his associate pastor through the adjoining door. "Ellis, Tick and I'll be in here. Can you put on coffee, the fancy kind for my friends?"

"I was telling Ticker about my sisters, Roof." Fox gestures at the pastor and says, "This annoying bloke is my only brother. We met in Columbus, Ohio, many years ago."

"Under questionable circumstances," Roofie chuckles. "Sit down, sit. The Parks and the Argalls go way back. Marley helps me with worship here. She brings Theiss every Wednesday and Sunday. Lots of fun. I encourage you both to join us anytime."

Fox slides his chair from the two men and stares at the door. "Gracie is lovely, of course. But her new thing is cooking 'authentic Cuban.' I explained it isn't really possible, but she appears to be going off on her own."

"I'm sure Grace appreciated your thoughts on the definition of authenticity." Roofie's eyes twinkle.

The detective frowns and shifts, flipping his thumbs over his phone. "I don't think she did, Roof. We expect the Gaffleys this weekend. Hope they can convince my wife about the food."

"Stel and I are invited, too," the pastor adds. "This party ought to be interesting."

"I think Tick's coming. Are you coming, Ticker? Probably

Skip and Sarah." Fox grimaces, eyes on his device. "Quite the crowd. Might be cluttered."

The pastor chuckles again as Jacob brings in a tray with ceramic mugs and fancy fixings.

"Why don't we talk about what's going on with your case?" Roofie asks, serving the drinks. "You two have a challenge. El, why don't you start?"

Fox stands and begins to wander in the small room. "I'll give it a go. I have a problem, rather, we have a problem." He doesn't say anymore.

Heat spikes in Tick's chest, and his back cramps. *Relax. One muscle at a time, start with your neck...*

Roofie allows the silence for a couple of minutes. "Guys, someone has to say words. Out loud words. Tick, how much have you been told about your present case?"

Fox moves to the window behind Roofie's chair, pacing in the tight space.

"I suspect Fox — Ellis..." Tick stops. "I suspect my lieutenant has more information than I do."

"What do *you* know?" Roofie leans across his desk.

"We found a bit of material in Stuart, at the Martin county sheriff's office. Fox saw what appeared to be blood and possibly meth. Methamphetamine. Thirty-six hours later, a similar piece of material was hanging from the railing at the top of the Inlet Light. There was a human lip."

"An upper lip," Fox adds.

Tick stiffens. "An upper lip, yes. A lot of blood. Too much blood for the lip itself to be the only source."

"About two, two and a half liters. A lot. Too much." The detective whispers, staring at his dark screen.

"Too much," Tick repeats, grinding his hands together. "The culprits tacked a military award on the sweater at the Inlet Light scene."

"An Army combat award." The Brick Breaker tune blares.

"Turn your phone down so we can hear your corrections or stop interrupting." Roofie swats the detective on his knee. "Go on, sergeant."

"Yes, technically, an Army combat award. The next day, after the scene at the Lighthouse, Fox picked me up in his personal car and drove us to Miami, to Jackson Memorial. Someone dumped a body at the Emergency Room doors. Marley was working the ER."

"I drive quite well." Fox pushes his forehead against the wooden window blind. The rattling echoes in the small room.

Roofie doesn't react to his friend. "Talk about the body in Miami."

"I didn't examine the body." Tick leans forward in his chair with a sigh. "Didn't enter the morgue. Somehow, it's connected to our case. My partner hasn't been forthcoming."

"Not accurate." Fox leaves the window and paces again, his phone flipping in his hand. His face contorts in anguish, driving panic into Tick.

"Shay, I'm sitting here in this weird meeting with your friend at his church because I'm not in the loop on this case. No offense, Pastor."

"Forthcoming implies a refusal to give information 'as promised.' I did not promise you the information. I specifically said 'No' when you asked me to explain."

"Fuck." Tick lays his head on his lap.

Roofie gets up and moves to the younger man, patting his shoulder. "El. Sit in my chair, and take The Lovely Yamaha. Play for us, your pick. Your choice of tune, not your choice to play. Come, now."

"I didn't say I'd explain. I said I would *not* explain."

"Ellis, play and talk to your partner. Tell him everything you can."

The detective slumps against the wall, flipping his phone from hand to hand. After a moment, he sits in Roofie's chair, resting the instrument on his knee. He begins 'I Surrender.'

"If only everyone understood your innate sense of humorous irony," Roofie laughs. "Tick, we'll be fine. Breathe and unclench your fists. Your partner and I have been down a few rough roads in our time. We'll go down this one together, the three of us. Trust will be a critical part of our journey. Finish, El. Tell us the rest."

"OK." Fox strums, humming. "Ticker, you're off The Sweater Case."

eleven
vacationing in detroit and other larks

"OFF THE CASE? What the hell? Why am I finding out in this church and not at the department?" Tick's face reddens. "This is out of line. You're off base, Lieutenant."

"Calm down, *Sergeant*." Fox isn't playing the guitar anymore, but he isn't looking up, either. "As Roofie said, you must trust me, as I trust you. The case has complications. Issues you don't need to be part of right now. Give me time, I've a plan. How much vacation do you have?"

"Vacation?" Tick drops his head, sinking onto his elbows in the chair. "Dammit, you're over-lording, not leading. This is why you brought me here, to your friend's church. Not acceptable."

"Ticker."

"No, man."

"This doesn't sound like trust." The detective plays the guitar again. "You're not listening."

"John," Roofie soothes. "Hear your partner out. You can still decide your path."

"I'm not here to be managed, Pastor." He flushes with rage, his knuckles white.

"No." Fox grinds his jaw. "So, here you go, John. Your

choice. Head back to the Department and talk to Cap. And apologize to Roofie."

"John, please listen to Ellis. Five minutes. No apologies necessary."

Tick plows his fist into the door. "Five minutes. Then I go to Cap."

Hurt flashes through Fox's pale eyes, and he flinches. "Five minutes. My sense of time is excellent. Evidence appears corrupted in this sweater case, and we need a path to untangle some of the threads. I need you to go to Detroit."

"Detroit?" Tick screams the word. "None of the shit you just spewed explains your behavior the last two days."

The detective sets the guitar down and turns away from the men. His lilt is heavy. "Detroit. Roofie will go with you to investigate the methamphetamine connection. The project I propose involves significant danger to you. I'm not sure I'm right. You ignore my stress. I'm working hard to maintain my balance. All this upsets me, too."

"Dammit—"

Roofie pats Tick's shoulder. "John, I have acquaintances close to the drug trade. We can find out what's going on. Ellis is trying to protect you."

"Protect me? I'm not a child to be sent to their room," Tick snarls. "How is Detroit in this picture? I'm off your official team, but you're fine with me going to Detroit, of all places, so I must be acceptable for that particular lark."

Fox taps his forehead on the wall. Moments pass before he speaks. "Hardly a 'lark,' my friend. Drugs have unique identifiers, including illegal drugs. Both mass spectrometry and nuclear magnetic resonance — you won't understand the science — can build a crumb trail back to the maker. Not perfect, of course. Indicators only. Our meth stain leads to Detroit."

The Sweater Case

"So, Charlie completed the tests on the sweater? Is she in on this conspiracy?"

"Of course, she isn't. She's not aware of my plan. I would never put Charlie at risk."

"But *my* risk is just hunky." Tick blows his breath out, rolling his shoulders.

"You're already at risk. Please pay attention. This is all for you. We need answers to mitigate your jeopardy. I believe those answers are in Detroit."

"My jeopardy."

"I have contacts in Detroit," Roofie repeats. "We may find some new information about the murder."

Tick sinks onto his elbows. "Fuck. Fuck. You arrogant ass. You speak in riddles and expect me to—"

"I'm not sharing everything with you. You decide if you trust me." Fox's voice cracks and he exhales. "I may have assessed our relationship incorrectly. I'll go to Detroit. You can help me if you'd take vacation days while I'm gone."

"Shit." Tick pushes his head back against the wall. "No, you didn't misunderstand our relationship. I'm caught off guard. Just give me a minute to adjust."

"Whoever goes will meet with one of the biggest liquid meth dealers in the country." Fox runs his fingers along the blinds, rattling them. "Ticker. I wish I could protect you, hide you in a safe place."

"Not sharing everything creates problems, not safety." The big man slumps, sliding down in the chair.

"Hence the trust. I can't remove the danger, sadly. You'll be under physical threat on the 'lark,' as you call it. Not to mention our captain's reaction when he finds out. Cap envisions himself as our protector, a father figure if you will. He doesn't like to be excluded. We must exclude him at this point, to protect him. He'll be very unhappy. He's a bit of a control freak."

Tick glances at Roofie, who gestures for silence.

Fox continues, "Take your vacation. I booked a hotel room in Detroit for tomorrow night. We have to book flights. Time is too short to drive."

"Not if we take off tonight and drive through. I want my car." Roofie walks back to his desk. "Tick? You in? Or am I taking Ellis?"

Nausea sweeps over Tick's face. "I'm in. I'm a fool, but I'm in."

"Take leave," Fox murmurs, visibly relaxing. "Avoid Cap. If you meet him, tell him your boss took you off the case. Don't hide your turmoil. Your obvious anguish will help us."

"I repeat. You're an asshole."

The detective plays 'Revelation Song.' "You aren't the first to say so."

twelve
place of shadows

THE ARGALL MASTER bedroom is dark and freezing cold.

How am I supposed to undress here without getting frostbite? Good grief.

Fox slips fully clothed under the covers, shivering. His wife is sound asleep. His shirt comes off easily enough, but his trousers catch on his feet. He wriggles to pull his cuffs off his ankles.

"What are you doing?" Grace murmurs.

"This room is sub-zero! How am I supposed to—" The last leg pops off, flipping backward and knocking his phone off the nightstand. He tries to toss his trousers on the chair, but they miss and land on the floor. "Arggh."

Grace rolls over and hugs her husband. "I'll keep you warm, Lad. Red Hots are warm." Her voice is a mumble.

"Ah, a wonderful idea." Fox reaches for his nightstand and the container of cinnamon candy. "How was your day? Mine was horrific."

"Mmm."

He shifts under the covers beside his wife and kisses her face, pulling her closer.

She's asleep. So much for my seduction talent. "I won't sleep for a while now," he whispers out loud to the cold room. He pulls the blanket up around his shoulders and starts a game of Brick Breaker.

Two hours later, Grace wakes him. "Honey, you're sleeping sitting up? You're ice cold!" She reaches up and rubs his chest and arms. "Hey, your fuzzy chest is muscley. This arm, too. Weight stuff with Tick? I like muscles."

"I'm freezing."

Grace kisses his side. "Frozen. But definitely muscley."

"My muscles did little for you last night," Fox grumbles.

"Last night...?" Her head is back on her pillow, her eyes closed. "Why don't you kiss me? I like muscley, fuzzy men."

"How many do you know, wife?" He snuggles down, gathering her in his arms, finding her mouth with his. She kisses him, then lays her head on his chest and goes back to sleep.

Menopause and Ambien. How I hate them.

When he awakens again, it's bright in the room. Sunlight is streaming in, bringing warmth. Grace walks out of the bathroom, dressed for work.

"Sleepyhead. You're late leaving. It's after seven." She sits on her husband's side of the bed, ruffling his curly hair and running her hand down his cheek. "Don't shave. I love you bristly."

"I'm avoiding Cap. No office for me. I've got to talk with Charlie."

"Avoiding Cap? I hope that's over by tomorrow. Cap and Sarah are coming to my Authentic Cuban Night." Grace giggles her fairy tinkle as her husband's eyes flash at the mention of the food. "I'll announce you believe all the food to be Pretend Cuban."

"Not 'pretend,' Gracie, but not 'authentic.' 'Authentic' means..."

The Sweater Case

She kisses him on the mouth. "I brushed my teeth. Minty! Hey! Your chest is muscley!" Her hands move under the covers.

"You're starting something. In fact, this would be the third time in the last few hours you started something you don't intend to finish." Fox sulks at his smiling wife.

"Third time?" Grace cocks her head, but continues to rub his chest and shoulders. "Seriously, like 1990 all over again, this chest and arms. When did this happen?"

"1990. Watch yourself, girlie."

She raises the sheet to peer at her husband's stomach, her beautiful blue eyes twinkling. "Do I spy a two-pack under here? Maybe all the other times were foreplay. I like foreplay."

"I have a three-pack," Fox answers, pulling his wife against him. "We're both going to be late for work."

"Charlie, can we talk?"

"Dr. Fox, we talk every day." The scientist smiles. "Several times a day. But, I understand you. Yes, we can talk. Let's go to my office. I'll make you my real Cuban coffee. We'll talk."

"Authentic coffee. Charlie, do you have plans for tomorrow? We're having a few friends over to the house, quite informal. Come by 1:00?"

"Ah, *si*, I would love to. Now, *que bola*?"

Fox looks at his shoes, shuffling. Moving to her friend's side, Charlie puts her arm through his and pulls him toward her office.

"*Asere. Dale,* we're fine, here. We know our young Tick. We will find the answers we need."

"Cap isn't informed of everything."

"Ah. *Por la izquierda.* A shock, you're always so predictable. This is a joke, of course."

"'To the left?' Is this expression sarcastic?"

"Yes, I'm being sarcastic. You often keep things from Cap."

"Do I? I don't— Well, usually to manage the information flow, to move slowly. Not to hide things."

"Well, my friend, I'm Latina. I like to do some things slowly, yes?" She narrows her eyes at the detective. "Captain Harley is your friend. He's highly capable. You often forget others' abilities."

"I never forget yours, dear Charlie."

She cants her head and smiles. "*Si*. You avoid my point, so we stay together in this place of shadows for a time. A short time, my friend, I warn you. Where do we go now?"

"I heard a curious thing yesterday. A deputy from Martin county implied the original scene was in Martin, not Palm Beach. Any data to suggest where the initial violence occurred? Or the timing of the crime?"

"Which crime? Several are possible. An event occurs and results in a person — our victim — vomiting with blood. I found no drugs in the vomitus. Then, a violent act causes more bloodshed from the same victim at the Inlet Light. The blood was fresh, indicating it came from a living body. The lip is a strange one. The excision wasn't fresh when discovered at the Jupiter scene. Hard to time the tissue degradation with south Florida sun and salt from the ocean rushing in and out of the inlet."

"They removed the lip post-mortem?"

"Peri-mortem. Yet, a timing issue. How is the excised lip not fresh, but also near death, and the blood fresh? I've no answer right now. I could use your head against it."

"OK, I'll ponder it. We can verify the excised lip matches the body from Jackson, yes?"

"Yes. That's clear."

Fox moves to the window and pulls his phone out, his

back to the scientist. He's silent for a few moments before he speaks. "But not a 'body,' Charlie. Dalia. The woman Tick pined over for months. Sweet Dalia."

"Well, here is another puzzle. Dalia is—was an RN at Jupiter Medical. They require hepatitis B vaccinations or a signed declination for employment in the hospital. We found no antibodies to hepatitis B, but no declination on record."

"Can we trust the records? Dalia's disappeared. Missing since we found the body. She left work the evening prior and didn't report the next day. I can't ask Tick. He's not aware of the situation. I sent him to Detroit last night."

"Detroit." Charlie moves to her desk and opens her computer. "This report I received? The nuclear magnetic resonance on the meth from the material shows indicators aligned with product coming from the Sinaloa cartel through San Ysidro into Wayne county, Michigan."

"As we suspected. I leapt ahead and sent them on."

"Them?"

"Roofie went with Tick."

"Ah, my Fox." Charlie shakes her head sadly. "What *are* you doing?"

The detective turns his back to Charlie, his voice grim. "Tick needs a firm hand. Roofie has a firm hand, and continued connections in both Wayne county and Gwinnett county in Georgia."

"Dear Fox. How will you live with yourself if anything happens to two of your most adored people?"

thirteen
define authentic

"I CAN HELP." Fox gazes out the window at the decorations in the Argall backyard. "The tables are uneven. Look at the chairs! Helter-skelter. Such a mishmash!"

"You're free to go move anything, Ellis Argall." Grace rolls her eyes and continues chopping tomatoes. "And while you're at it, think of how to keep your boss and Stel separated. What will you say to Cap when he learns of The Lark to Detroit? Want to experience a real mishmash? Just wait."

"Cap hasn't met Stel," he snorts. "They're strangers to each other. Why would he ask her anything? Do people do that?"

"Ask about others' families? A shock, but yes. They do."

"Pssh. Never noticed such a thing." He finishes putting his shoes on and heads out the door.

"Another shocker," Grace murmurs to herself as her husband drags the tables across their backyard.

━━

"We can't discuss work here, Fox. Our wives would both do us harm if we did." Cap stands near the fence as the guests mingle in the small space. "But can we confirm the identity of the Sweater Case victim?"

"Not yet. We can't find any relatives. No one to bring in for an identification. No one to notify, and we want to avoid involving anyone at the Medical Center. Only been a day and a half."

"You told Tick about it all?" Cap regards his subordinate, eyes narrow. "You two discussed the complications?"

"He's on vacation, and it wasn't imperative to tell him before he left."

"Your partner is unaware he's off the case?" Cap's wife motions for his attention and he misses the momentary struggle on his lieutenant's face.

"Did you tell him?" Fox is head down, playing Brick Breaker.

"No, I didn't run into him last night. Thought he'd be here."

"Gentlemen! Who wants a fresh drink?" Ez Gaffley strolls up to the men, carrying a bottle and three glasses. "Bourbon is not the drink for today, *mis amigos*. Rum, please, to favor the atmosphere."

"Ez, did you speak with Grace about this 'authentic' thing?" Fox frowns. "I tried to explain, but she's going her own way."

"A conversation best saved for Charlie." Ez smiles at Cap, who chuckles. "Drink, *amigo*. We will live a long day tomorrow at the clinic. Today is to relax, not educate wives. I've found they don't like it. I avoid unsettling my equilibrium. *Tremendo paquete*."

"Accuracy is important. Sometimes drama serves as a sacrifice to honesty. You know, clear the air." The detective's thumbs are flipping away at his game. "Like how I enjoy my friends, but not the mishmash chaos in this yard."

"Honesty." Stella Parks stalks across the yard, glaring up at

Fox. "Let's clear the air about honesty, Ellis Argall. Then we can talk about real chaos." She pushes her face into his, her hands fisted and pale.

"Stel. Stella, pet. Have you met Ez Gaffley?" Fox's brows flash up, and he bobbles his phone before dropping it.

Stella stomps on the device with a loud crack, crushing it into the grass. "Has Ez Gaffley met *you*? I doubt it!" She raises her hand to slap the detective before grasping control. Her eyes fill with tears, and she whirls away, rushing past the men and out the gate.

"Crikey." Fox stares at the broken phone. When he glances up, Grace is watching him from across the yard.

Cap finishes his drink. "Wives appear to be a theme at this party. Roofie Parks' wife is *cynddrwg iawn* [very angry], Lieutenant. I wonder if it's to do with her husband's vacation with Ticker to Detroit? *Rydych yn mynd i gael diwrnod garw heb eich ffon.* You're going to have a rough day without your phone. The Department isn't paying for a new one."

fourteen
detroit: fear is a competitive sport

"REVEREND PARKS, OUR FRIENDSHIP IS STALE." Robert Alvarez leans back in his black leather, ergonomic desk chair.

Roofie and Tick stand in an elegant, window-lined corner office on the 14th floor in a high-rise building overlooking the Detroit River.

Tick works to relax and keep his eyes on Alvarez. *His chair is like something from a spaceship. What does this place cost every month?*

"Stale?" Roofie walks behind Alvarez, placing his arm over the back of the chair. "How did it happen, Robby?"

Alvarez snorts. "We've all moved on. I've moved on."

"Like with this jumped-up chair?" Roofie laughs.

The man flinches, but his voice is neutral. "A Herman Miller Aeron. Like? I'll send you one. Old times."

"Nah, I'm good. Robby, man. I'm not interested in your business. Not connecting anything to you. I'm trying to understand how meth from Detroit landed a dead girl in my yard."

"You standin' right here, brother. Sounds like you connectin' two things. You ain't nowhere else."

"Unless you killed this girl, I'm not *connectin'* anything." Roofie leans closer to Robert and lowers his voice. "You kill this girl?"

Alvarez stands up and turns into Roofie, moving him back until he touches the expansive windows. Tick tightens up and steps to the desk.

The man presses the pastor against the glass and snarls, "Your boy here a threat to me, Roof?"

Seconds pass in thick tension until Roofie murmurs, "No. This is a friendly meeting. Tick's a friend. We're trying to stay out of this mess. Not go further in."

"Here's my old home tip, *friend*. You need to understand it's for your mama and auntie. Our young *friend* here *is* the mess."

Tick sways in shock. *I'm the mess?*

"Thanks, but we don't need old news." Roofie's voice is calm.

"I'm giving you a two-minute warning. Take this kid out of Detroit." Alvarez returns to his fancy chair, shoulders stiff. "Don't come back."

"One more for Mama, Robby. I'll have her send you and your mom an invite to dinner at Christmas. Why is Tick the mess? Because I'll tell you sure, he's innocent here."

Robert relaxes and laughs. "Innocent? What the fuck is innocent? My mom eats with your mama every Sunday afternoon. We don't need no special invitations."

"Robby. Give me one next step."

"You both head to my door and if you want to talk to me, you limit your visits to the east side of Columbus at Christmas with witnesses. Don't show up here again." Alvarez waves the men out.

"You're afraid," Roofie challenges.

"Afraid? You're fucking right, I'm afraid. You're so far gone, Roof. Even when you were in it, you never got it. In my work, fear is a competitive sport. Here?" He swings his arms to encompass the room. "Here, I'm only worried about losing my life. Where you two are playing, you risk your life and all your money. Your family. You lose the legacy. I've worked too hard to give everything away for a stupid kid I never met."

"Everything," the sergeant murmurs.

"That's right, punk. You've got out-sized enemies. I don't play with the District."

Tick jerks before he can stop, bringing a smirk to Alvarez's hard mouth.

"You didn't know, kid? Well, Roof, my gift to you. Now walk out."

"What just happened, Roofie?" Heat flashes through Tick. "The District? Did he mean DC?"

"He did." The pastor pulls Tick toward their car, which is parked in the alley behind Alvarez's office. Two men follow them out. "Get in the car. We need to be on the road."

"On the road?" Tick's voice rises. "On the road to where? What the fuck is going on?"

One of the men calls out. "Reverend Parks?"

Roofie turns, but Tick yanks on his arm. "Are you nuts? Come on."

"No, Tick." Roofie walks back to the man. "I'm Reverend Parks."

"You the singer, right? Damn, oh. I'm sorry. I mean, I saw you sing on TV. Stopped my heart, man. Your voice, whoa. That voice." The man shakes his head and timidly says, "I sing."

"You sing? My young friend, I don't sing. I worship. Do you worship?"

The young man drops his head. "Nah, man. No."

"I can teach you. Come visit me in Jupiter, Florida. Anytime." Roofie pats the man on the shoulder and shakes his hand. "I mean it. Come and we'll worship together."

Returning to Tick, the pastor says, "Keep walking. Time to go." The two men continue to follow them into the alley.

Roofie opens the passenger side door to his car and tosses the keys to Tick. "Your turn to drive. South Florida is a long way. Wave goodbye to our friends."

As the car turns from the alley, Roofie holds up a tiny, square, folded piece of paper. "Our singer gave us a gift."

"Grab an evidence bag out of my jacket on the back seat. Your friend Ellis never has one. Bag the note after you read it."

The note is folded in an intricate puzzle, like the ones the girls passed in junior high. Neat writing in blue ink says:

Chuck Sams, atty.

Roofie holds the paper for Tick to read.

"Attorney? Never heard of him."

"I haven't, either. I suspect he works in the District of Columbia. I'll try to search for him. Might be hard if this name is a nickname, you know, Chuck. Might be Charles." Roofie fumbles with his phone. "I was wrong. It's Chuck. Chuck Sams. He works in Boston, Massachusetts. For a law firm I'm familiar with — Masters, Griffin, and Larkin."

"Why does the law firm name sound familiar?" Tick asks.

"Masters was Ellis' firm when he practiced law in Boston. Tom Masters, the senior partner, is the lawyer who represented the murderous pedophile Conway in his divorce."

"I'll never forget him. He almost ruined my partner."

fifteen
control freak

FOX SPRAWLS in a deep brown leather chair in his library, long legs on a striped hassock. The Authentic Cuban party continues outside, Latin music and jumbled voices in the background.

"Do you want a drink? I want one. At least." Cap pours two glasses of bourbon, handing one to his lieutenant. "I'm working hard not to kick your Welsh ass."

"This footstool is ugly. Grace insisted on buying it. How did you find out about Detroit? Charlie tell you?" Fox sighs, looking at his empty hands before accepting the drink. "I need my phone."

"My love for your wife is the only reason I'm not committing a felony."

"My love for you is the only reason I'm protecting you. At the risk of repeating myself, how did you learn about the trip to Detroit?"

Cap leans into his detective's face and snarls. "Well, it's weird. I got a hit on a car — Roofie's car — going through the Florida Turnpike tolls. My buddy in West Virginia picked him up again. I had Bret in Charleston take a gander at the passenger and driver. Lo, a toll picture with two handsome dudes, both of whom I recognized. Tick looked very stressed."

"I'm certain of it. You put out a call on Roofie. I understand you're angry. *Beth mae hyn yn mynd i gostio?*" [What's this going to cost me?]

"Do you care what your micromanaging is going to cost Tick?"

Fox swirls his drink, exhaling. "My partner is on vacation. He's free to travel wherever he'd like, isn't he?"

"Ellis Cadnon 'The Fox' Argall, the Chess Master. What would your beloved mentor Mac say about the callous finagling of your subordinate?" Cap throws back his drink and pours another. "You fucking exhaust me. I'm not sure you're worth it."

"Tick has to play a role here, Skip. He can't be left out."

"You do *not* make that decision."

"You give me too much credit. I didn't make it. Tick's a grown lad. He can decide his own path."

Cap's face darkens, his voice rising. "So, he's aware you examined the body, and the body is his girlfriend? You told him Charlie found his DNA on the military award? You haven't 'left him out' of anything? By the way, why don't you mention the driver's license?"

"The license is my point. This is too amateurish to be a serious frame-up. Everywhere we turn, some minor item implicates Tick. No real forensic pattern exists or is forming."

"The outdated license is actually our best evidence, but you kept it from me. The license all but proves this whole thing is a frame. You're not thinking. You're putting your partner at risk."

"Tick's reaction to Dalia's murder is the risk."

"So that's a 'no'? You don't trust me or your partner, so we're out of your personal Batman fantasy loop? He's not aware he's now a suspect and I'm forced to bring him in for questioning? His 'vacation' will be viewed as possible flight, dammit! If we connect this murder to meth trade from—well, any fucking where—the feds have every right to ask why they haven't been called in. And my sergeant is in Detroit for some damn reason I can't fucking explain."

"He's not acting as an officer. No one's pulling badges."

"How the hell do you know what anyone is doing in fucking Detroit?" Cap roars, slamming his drink on a glass side table, splintering both pieces. Bourbon splashes everywhere and blood pours from several cuts in his hand. "Shit! SHIT!"

Fox jumps up as Cap flings his hand around, cursing. "Hold still, Skipper. Let me examine your hand."

"I don't want you looking at it! Get Ez!" Cap shouts, gritting his teeth and squeezing his fist shut.

"Stop balling up your hand. You may have glass shards in your palm. Ez is a pathologist. He isn't your best bet here."

"And the fucking lawyer is? No thanks!" Cap storms toward the door and runs straight into Ez. *"Damniwch y cyfan!"* [Damn it all!]

"You're drawing negative attention, *compadres*. I remind you of the equilibrium I savor." Ez gestures to the blood running down Cap's arm. "Well, we have no peace here, I see. Give me your arm and hand. We must assess the damage."

"Fuck!" The senior officer bellows, holding his elbow.

"Dr. Argall, you have a medical kit here?" The medical examiner eases open the captain's fingers. "Of course, you do. We will care for your captain. Skip, you must sit."

Fox pulls a medical kit from a drawer and lays out a folding table of medical materials, including a syringe he fills from a vial. "I'm going to anesthetize the area and put in stitches. Will you hold still? Let me explain. I'm thinking of Tick—every minute. And of you, *annwyl ffrind*. [dear friend] Roofie has contacts in Detroit. I needed Tick gone, Skipper. He can't learn of our suspicions until we confirm the identity of the body."

He stitches up three deep cuts on Cap's palm. "My stitching is much better than a pathologist's — their work doesn't require precision, and we want limited scarring here. Dead bodies don't scar. Tell him, Ez."

"Dr. Argall is correct, of course. His work is quite *perfecto*. One would expect obsessive neatness, yes?"

"I may be able to help with the identity of the victim." Charlie Perez leans against the door to the library. "I'm also an excellent stitcher. More of a hobby."

The men look up at the forensic scientist, who waits for their full attention.

"The body is Dalia's twin. Her identical twin."

Fox blinks and cocks his head to the side. "Then where is Dalia?"

sixteen
georgia has swamps, right?

"SO, WE HEADED TO—WHERE?" Tick sits upright in the passenger side of Roofie's car, rolling his shoulders.

"Breathe, man. We're headed back to Jupiter. We meet with Fox and the rest of your team. Bring the picture up to date. I'm planning a side trip. I want to visit another old friend in north Georgia off I-75."

"Is this an actual friend?"

"You're too smart to ask such a question. When our old friends are acting out in ways we left behind, like in my case, they'll be tense when we meet again. Robby Alvarez helped us out. Look, he's living a dangerous life. One I wish he would leave, but he must choose."

Tick squirms in his seat, turning sideways to face the pastor. "You sold drugs at that level?"

"Pssh. Put your cop back in the holster." Roofie glances at his passenger. "You saying your past is clean? It's not where you came from, Tick. It's not where you are right now. The only important thing is where you're headed. Remember. Let's not go there."

Tick groans, sinking into his seat. "Hard not to go there. Drugs destroyed my neighborhood growing up. Both drug use and the dream of becoming rich and powerful by selling them. I fought every minute to keep my younger brother with a top-notch brain away from all the nonsense."

"I understand your feelings up close and personal. The destruction from the gangs and drugs in our neighborhoods is heartbreaking. I also value my experience. My life was redeemed. Too much focus on blame and you miss the only path out of the storm. We'll be working with damaged people, Sergeant. Let's keep our eyes on what we want."

Roofie's phone rings. "Hey, Ellis, you're on speaker."

"Tick's with you?"

"Yeah, I'm here. Who's with you?"

"No one. I'm all alone. You're stopping in Gwinnett?"

Tick drops his head and growls. "Everyone's talking about everything to everyone except me." He grinds a white-knuckled fist into his leg. "I'm fucking done—"

"I'll change it now." Fox interrupts, his voice neutral. "I'm reading you in on the entire case to date. Big stuff first. The body in the morgue is Dalia's twin. She had an outdated driver's license belonging to you in her back pocket. Do you need me to stop for questions?"

Tick's face drains.

"Go ahead, El. We're listening," Roofie urges.

"I didn't tell Cap about certain items in a timely manner. But I'll argue the delay was only a few hours. I needed time. I also needed the time with you not being in the loop, Ticker. Your involvement would create an environment we didn't want."

"*We.*" Tick shakes his head.

"*We* are in a swamp. Swamps are no place for tea and holding hands. We must be ready to move quickly, and you have to trust my loyalty to you. Now, back to chronological order on the case summary. The DNA on the sweater from Martin county shares DNA with the Jackson ER body, but we didn't have an identity at the time. After seeing the body, we proceeded with the hypothesis the body was Dalia through my visual ID alone. Questions?"

"No." Tick's voice is flat.

"The military award on the Inlet Light had your DNA on it. Quite a bit. It's an Army combat ribbon, and you received the same one in service. So the working hypothesis is it belongs to you. I left some detail out of the initial reporting to you and Cap to gain time. Cap has all the information now. He's aware you're with Roofie and in Detroit. We had a—an interaction at the house yesterday evening."

"An interaction?" Tick rolls his shoulders and unclenches his hands.

"Cap has stitches and Stel is not my friend. Luckily, Grace saw it all coming somehow and was prepared. She isn't happy, but still loves me."

Roofie grimaces at Tick, who groans.

"Ah, well, cracked eggs and soufflés," the detective murmurs. "The blood found at the Lighthouse scene and the DNA from the sweater at Martin county matches the body dumped at Jackson Memorial. Anomalies between Dalia and the body indicated a need for a deeper examination. For example, an absence of Hepatitis B antibodies was a flag. Vaccines are required for all RNs, so we expected to find the antibodies. We didn't. Questions?"

"Where is Dalia?" Tick asks.

"That's the question I asked. No answers. Dalia has disappeared."

Anguish flows over Tick's face. "How are you so sure this is her twin? I'm unaware of a twin or any family. What if this is a mistake?"

"Charlie did the work herself. When you're back in Jupiter, she can explain how genetically identical people are actually different. Suffice it for now: a number of those differences signaled questions. One significant question was weight. This body was undernourished and lacked the muscle expected in Dalia. Unexpected cardiac issues. The vaccine antibodies, or lack thereof. Drugs were present in hair. Meth, but also heroin. I identified her in a sheet, face only, but even if I'd seen her body, I was unlikely to notice these points. We'll leave the rest for later. We're sure about the identity."

"But Dalia—"

"Ticker. To find Dalia, we follow the trail of her twin. Trust me, we'll establish a connection. The chance it's not connected is so low as to be unworthy of examination."

Roofie reaches for Tick's arm. "Any questions?"

The sergeant shakes his head.

"We follow the meth trail," Roofie says. "We're headed for Fuzzy Whalin in Gwinnett."

"Call me when you make it to Gwinnett." Fox disconnects.

Silence fills the car as the men head south on Interstate 75.

"Roofie, what about the folded paper? The Boston connection?"

"Our mutual detective friend isn't the only one who needs to manage the timing of information. The name on the paper is likely to bring distractions we can't afford right now."

"So we ignore it?" The heat flies up through Tick's chest into his face. "You two are cut from the same cloth, aren't you?"

"I promise you, the Boston branch of the trail won't stay hidden for long. In fact, I hope to understand better after we visit Georgia."

"I hope we understand a lot of things better after we visit Georgia."

seventeen
frenemies aren't a real thing

"GRACIE! DID YOU MAKE COFFEE?" Fox calls from the bedroom. "I'll make it from the new beans Tick brought. Whole beans. He gave them to me before he got mad. A grinder, too. Your breakfast boyfriend thinks coffee is 'most definitely' not all the same."

He walks to the empty kitchen, jumping on one foot as he puts on a sock. "Grace!"

Did she go outside?

The door between the kitchen and garage stands open.

"Wife, you air-conditioning the garage now?" The passenger door in her car is open. She isn't in the car.

Where is she?

He heads out the kitchen door, scanning the fenced backyard. Grace is standing in the alley, talking to a woman.

Ann Carley.

"Grace! You left all the doors open." He stares at the Martin county deputy, twisting his second sock in his hand.

The two women's eyes drop from his bright scarlet workout shorts to his single-socked foot.

Flushing pink, Grace says, "Honey, this is Ann Carley. She's in my book club. We meet at The Jersey Diner on

Wednesday night. She's new to our group. Ann, meet my husband, Fox."

The deputy smiles and extends her hand. "I've heard a lot about you."

Fox frowns and blinks. "Hello again, Ann. Or shall I say Deputy Carley?"

"Again?" Grace looks between the two. "You've met?"

"Your husband and I met recently. We're on a Palm Beach-Martin county task force together. I'm a deputy sheriff in Martin county."

"If you don't mind, can you tell me why you're here?" The detective waves his hand. "In our alley?"

"I bought the house two doors down on the right. Well, not 'bought' yet. They accepted my offer this morning."

"Oh, that's wonderful!" Grace turns to the woman, her eyes sparkling. "This is a fabulous neighborhood. All the Abacoa development is lovely and so convenient. Isn't it wonderful, honey? Another law enforcement officer in the vicinity."

Fox shifts in his odd dance, his hands thrust low into his pockets. "I need to go pick up my new phone. Welcome to the neighborhood, Deputy Carley."

"You were so rude! So embarrassing. Sometimes, I just—despair of—what were you thinking? Is this about your phone?" Grace sits beside her husband on the walnut four-poster bed dominating their master bedroom.

Fox stretches out on the bed, watching a Miami Marlins game and playing on his new phone. "Who chooses to pay Palm Beach county property taxes to drive an hour to Stuart? Her office is off Highway One an hour away, anyway you travel."

"What?" Grace glares. "Taxes? What? Ann was probably embarrassed, too."

"We're talking about a half-million-dollar home. She's a deputy sheriff in a county with much lower taxes. How does she afford it?"

"Ellis Argall! How can you say such a thing? *We* live here. What are you going on about? How is her house any of your business?"

"Were you in your car? In the garage?"

"What? Fox…"

"The car, Gracie. Did you open the passenger door before you went into the alley?"

"No. I wasn't in the garage. I was weeding the sideyard as Ann walked past. Explain this interrogation to me?"

He pulls her to him and lays his head in her lap. "Aw, darling girl. I'm knackered. This Tick thing, everyone is all dramatic. I'm uniquely incapable of dealing with drama. Come here and kiss me. Calm me down."

"No way." She runs her fingers through his hair. "Crazy head. I'm going to collect our granddaughter. The kids are going to a movie, and I'm late. Besides, I'm still angry."

"You can't be mad. You think I'm cute."

"*You* think you're cute. *I'm* sure I'm irritated."

"See? Drama. It's everywhere. An invasion of emotional outrage. A torrent."

She pushes him away, flipping her hand in the air. "You're incorrigible. Your baby Theiss and I'll be in the kitchen in an hour. Come eat ice cream with us, and we'll act like normal people."

Fox waits until the garage door closes, picks up his phone, and punches in a number. "Cap. I've a problem here. Can we meet at the department?"

"I agree with Grace about Deputy Carley. This is likely a coincidence." Cap unlocks his door on the Violent Crimes floor, waving his lieutenant into the shadowed office. "Abacoa's a lovely place. Carley might be married to a scientist at the Scripps research facility, or maybe she inherited money. Not unheard of for sheriff deputies to collect a string of advanced degrees. Might be her third career."

"Very funny. She's barely thirty years old. Mathematically, even I couldn't do such a thing. What about the car door?"

"Doctor, bring the first aid kit from the cabinet next to you and change this bandage. *Rwy'n credu eich bod yn ddyledus i mi.*" [I think you owe me.] He pulls a bottle of Blanton's from the long cabinet behind his desk and pours two glasses. "Do the medical stuff before you drink."

"*Daw adfyd gyda chyfarwyddyd yn ei law.* 'Adversity comes with instruction in his hand.' Technically, *you* owe *me*. Slamming crystal glasses on fragile, antique tables may not be a best practice. I'm properly concerned about this woman. Another proverb: 'Never trust overmuch a new friend or an old enemy.'"

"Welsh pessimism. We've had a few rough days. Tick's an anchor for you, and he's being threatened. I'm sure your partner is surly. Fortunately, Roofie has to manage him. I'm over my delicate detectives." Cap leans back in his maroon chair and sips his drink. "Myself, I wrote your severance letter twice."

Fox rolls his eyes and spins in one of the leather guest chairs in front of Cap's massive desk. "How do your orchids make it through the weekends? Isn't the humidity quite precise?"

"What's a weekend? Each orchid container has pebbles to support a constant humidity level. I maintain water at an exact mark."

Cap carries the drinks around his desk to Fox, handing the

detective his glass. "How is it I always come to you? Now, change my bandages, Dr. Argall. When are the runaways due back? Don't dissemble. Remember my spies."

"You don't seem angry with me anymore."

"Read a fascinating book last night about dealing with assholes at work. I'm using other tactics with you. Plus, I'm tracking your renegades through tolls. I know exactly where they are at all times." The captain pulls a folding table between the two chairs and lays his palm up. "Fix me."

Fox removes the bandages and examines the stitches. "I've instructed my colleagues to come back through Cincinnati on I-75 and to avoid the Express Lanes. Only the Express is under a toll. This repair is lovely, brilliant. I think despite your age, we'll have almost no visible scarring."

"Asshole. Other people don't get you, but I do."

The detective winks and raises his glass. "Here's to no one else discovering."

eighteen
checkers is a distraction, not a strategy

THE ARGALLS LIE ENTWINED in shadows on their bed, the moon still shining through their white cottage shutters.

"Your hair tickles," Fox murmurs into Grace's curly red hair, stroking his wife's thigh. "And getting gray. Kinda fading from when we were kids. Don't spend any time sussing it out. Simple biologic functionality of the eumelanin as you grow old."

"Thanks, Dr. Argall." The flare in her blue eyes goes unnoticed. "Where are you headed?"

"Stan Baskins and I are going to Georgia first, and we may end in DC, Boston, or both. If we have to go north, we'll fly out of Atlanta. I'll call. I'll be gone no more than a couple of days. You're not to worry."

"So finally bringing in the FBI. Are they looking at Tick?"

"Not yet, but moments away. Palm Beach can keep the murder for a while. A few specks of meth on a piece of sweater may be incidental. Once we establish the connection to drugs trade, it's federal. If I fail to pull Tick out, well. Cap'll have his work cut out for him." Fox frowns, squirming, and reaches for his phone.

The Sweater Case

What will he do if he loses Tick? What will any of us do? Nausea accompanies the sudden awareness of the young sergeant's importance to her husband. A successful partnership eluded him until now, fifteen years into his police career.

"I love you, Lad. Please eat while you're gone."

"You do love me, and I'll never deserve it."

"You ignored the 'please eat' part." She rubs her hand across her husband's stomach. "Well, you're all muscley now."

"I'm glad it helps." His green eyes twinkle. A vague smile rises to his lips, but he's already in Brick Breaker, his electronic hideyhole.

I live outside his gate. Does the challenge excite me or hurt me? Or is it a relief? All three, often at the same time.

"Wife. Don't you women use some beastly dye?"

"Isn't it time for you to go to work?" She flings her legs off the bed. "You shower first, and I'll make Tick's coffee."

Cap pulls his ID out to swipe the door to Violent Crimes, almost stumbling over Fox. The detective sits in a darkened area beside the elevators playing on his phone. "Dammit, why didn't you go in?"

"I rarely beat you here. Grace is moody. Irritated."

"Well, shit. That portends irritation all around." Cap unlocks the door. "Stay out."

Fox follows his boss, his eyes on his device. "I'm heading out with Stan Baskins to Gwinnett county. Lead the feds off Tick's scent."

Whirling around, Cap walks back and glares at his lieutenant. "What is this, a freaking private investigator noir novel? You Mike Hammer, now?"

The detective snickers, missing the sarcasm. "Always

thought I looked a bit like Armand Assante, without the odd mouth thing."

"Dr. Argall." Cap pokes his finger into Fox's tie. "You miss my point. Don't play half-ass with our local FBI agent. Subterfuge is not your strong suit. Too much time alone with Stan could be disastrous. Have you bothered to read his background? You're screwing up if you think you can lead him. *Ffycin uffern.*" [Fucking hell.]

"You worry unnecessarily. We need Stan for the federal reach into the meth connection — your idea, I believe." Concern flashes across his face. "Are you merked because your hand hurts? Have you done something to it? Let me examine the repair before I leave. I'm sure it's not infected. My procedure was perfect."

"No, my hand doesn't hurt. I'm fucking merked with your blasé attitude to driving the countryside with the FBI when we're trying to avoid federal attention!"

"Would you prefer I be nervous? This confuses me."

"Of course not." Cap leans across his desk at his lieutenant. "Your emotional state is not my point."

"Skipper. *Your* emotional state is *my* point." Fox lowers his phone and meets his supervisor's scowl, shifting his feet. "We agreed we need the FBI."

"Yes," Cap exhales. "Yes. We need the FBI. But remember the stakes here. I'm bringing Tick in for questioning as soon as he enters Palm Beach county. And he better arrive today or I'm sending a car for him."

"It worries you to send a car for him." Fox moves his phone from one hand to another as he struggles to stand still.

"It should worry you!"

"Umm... Skip. This is different for me. Your responsibility to order a wonderful young man picked up and embarrassed upsets you."

"Mae pobl normal yn poeni am deimladau eraill." [Normal people care about other people's feelings.]

"Fair play. I remind you, I'm not *your* normal. The evidence shows Ticker's in the clear. I don't have to hide his guilt. Stan and I have the same goal." Fox frowns again, tilting his head. "I play chess, not checkers. The single events are just data points, leading to the ultimate checkmate. You fear Tick's reaction to being questioned, so your emotions force you to over-value the single event and think short term. You're playing checkers."

"You need to leave before I get myself fired."

"I'll call you. I promise." Fox walks out, already back in his game.

"Can't wait."

nineteen
majoring in the minors

"STAN, been a while. How's federal encroachment going? I trust invading and imposing on sovereign states is still a delight?" Fox throws a soft football block and knocks the other man off balance.

They stand in the parking area of the Palm Beach county sheriff's department, beside the FBI agent's navy blue Lexus.

The detective runs his hand across the hood. "Feds give better cars."

Stan Baskins smiles at his colleague. "You, too can have a nice car. No one at the bureau understands how a control freak like you wouldn't jump at our offers to bring you in. I told them you were a Welsh radical individualist, but they persist. Methamphetamine, huh?"

"It appears so, but I warn you, a small enough amount to have been incidental to a benign interaction. Still, I value your drugs expertise."

"I sincerely doubt it, Dr. Argall," Stan chuckles. "I strongly suspect you value my federal facilitation, but here I am, anyway. How's Grace? Marley and gang?"

"My wife is a revelation, as always. My daughter and crew are off doing their own thing. Theiss is with us a lot; Marley's finishing her residency in emergency medicine soon. And yours, my friend?"

"My girlfriend Calley and I broke it off. Police work wasn't her idea of a life."

"You're young. Many fish."

"How many fish did you catch and throw back?" Stan sighs. "Nah, I may have to choose between a marriage and my career."

"Never so. The right girl will be the right girl. Patience. Like in this case. I warn you. Some complexities, and not jumping to conclusions will be a benefit."

"Sounds like a leading statement, Counselor. Am I to be privy to these complexities soon, or will you dole them out like rewards for good behavior?"

"You like to drive, yes?" Fox opens the passenger door and gets in the dark sedan, his phone out.

Stan shakes his head before dropping into the driver's seat. "Oh yeah, I love to drive. Nothing like I-95 in SoFla."

"Let's go turnpike. I think it will be less congested."

An hour into their trip, a text pops up on Fox's phone from a blocked number, covering his game.

> "Port St. Lucie rest area. Women's bathroom. Dump your partner."

"Hey, Stan, I need a quick stop to make a phone call. Port St. Lucie is coming up. Mind?"

"Nah, of course not." The agent narrows his eyes at his passenger. "Bring me in on your message?"

"No, but I admit it may be interesting to us both. Give me some space. You can trust me."

"Eventually, you can be trusted. The question is how many machinations I endure before you grace me with your Sherlockian wisdom."

The detective doesn't raise his head from his game. "Sherlock was British and not particularly collegial. Poor Watson."

"Oh, yes. Poor Watson. Speaking of side-kicks, where's Tick?"

"Ticker is on a well-deserved vacation. In fact, he's probably passing us on I-95 south on his way home as we drive north."

The men drive into the turnpike rest area. A lone truck sits at the south entrance to a deserted parking lot, orange barrels on the open tailgate and on the concrete below.

"Where are the cars?" Stan slows to a stop. "I expected more vehicles."

Fox points to a line of palms on the north corner. "Can you drop me at the building and park in the shade under those trees? Give me fifteen minutes and I'll be back."

"You get a secret text, and now you're going inside a weirdly abandoned rest stop without your backup?"

"For a conversation only, agent. Trust me. Give me fifteen minutes." Fox exits the car and leans back in, smiling. "I'm a professional."

"Your disarming grin doesn't fool me. I, too, am a professional. Don't walk into trouble. You'll pull me in with you."

"Agent Baskins. I'm famous for avoiding trouble."

"The exact polar opposite of the actual truth, Dr. Argall."

"Way too many adjectives. One-quarter of an hour." Fox walks into the expansive lobby of the building, which is devoid of people.

A snack dispenser is on the east wall next to a small opening marked 'Family Restroom.' Two additional toilet areas cover the west wall, separated by a closet. A 'restroom closed' sign hangs on a bright pink rope between orange cones in front of the women's area.

A janitor steps out of the closet carrying a silver bucket.

Fox approaches the woman and shows his badge. "No

worries, please," he says, in a thick Welsh accent. "Just a routine check."

She doesn't answer.

"Firenza. Beautiful name." He leans into his lilt.

The woman nods but stays silent as the detective steps past the cordon into the woman's toilet area.

The bathroom's lights are off, and if there is an auto light, it doesn't come on.

He smells her before he sees her.

"You simply can *not* change, can you, dear Ellis? Throwing your charm around like a fog to cover your footsteps. The enthralled are left positively dizzy until the magic floats away and they finally notice you stole their purse."

Natalie Forester walks out of a stall, dressed in a slick green silk dress. Her dark hair shines in the shadows as she leans against the sink. "Or shall I call you Fox? I think it's much sexier. Lustful, in a way. Fox."

"Natalie."

Laughing, she lowers her voice to almost a whisper. "So difficult to read you, doctor-lawyer-policeman. Have I succeeded in surprising you? I wanted to surprise you."

"What do you want?"

She waves her hands around the restroom. "I mean, really. The depths to which I stoop to entertain you."

"What do you want?" Fox repeats.

"What I always want, Ellis. What I've wanted since the memorable American Healthcare Lawyers' Conference in Baltimore, so many years ago. To help you is my only desire." Natalie primps in the mirror, touching her dark red lip. "We've both aged well."

"Plastic lives forever."

"Ouch! I'm scorched. Shattered. You aren't interested in how your sweet John Tickman got into so much... Muck?"

Her beautiful nose wrinkles. "Or should I just say blood? Goodness. Such a mess."

"You obstruct my investigation and I'll arrest you."

"Oh, dear. You and I are exquisite lawyers. Are you reverting to caveman policing instincts? Too long on the force?" Natalie takes a step toward the detective and stops, her eyes glinting. "You need to listen, Dr. Argall. I'm your only hope."

"A line from a badly written novel. I struggle to understand why you have any involvement in anything remotely connected to my partner."

"Dear Ellis. Nothing is connected to your Tick. This is all about you. And you, my friend, are majoring in the minors, as we say. Detroit? And oh. Lawd." Flashing beautiful white teeth, she sneers in a contrived southern accent. "Gwin-nett County? Please."

"OK, Natalie. Not meth. What, then?"

"Meth, of course. The tool is certainly methamphetamine. I remind you, knowledge is power and power is precious."

"Can we stop playing games before the FBI appears?"

"Yes, your over-qualified chauffeur. He's well-attended. Here's a fact set to redirect you. I remember a brilliant attorney who always said, 'Never play checkers when your enemy plays chess.' Here is the checkers distraction: meth trails. The chess direction? Who reported the bloody sweater at the Inlet Light? Your move." Natalie sweeps past him and out of the restroom in a waft of woody perfume.

Fox slumps against the grimy tiled wall, suddenly out of breath. *I spoke to The Colony family about the Lighthouse sweater myself. What did I miss?*

"Fox?" Stan storms into the opening. "What the hell are you doing? A freaking lunatic security guard harangued me for twenty minutes! He refused my ID and talked endlessly about reported sexual predators. I couldn't get a word in edgewise."

"Did a woman pass you?" The detective lays his head back again, closing his eyes.

"A woman? No, a paunchy middle-aged guy, a turnpike security guard."

"We need to leave."

A janitor's uniform is on the floor outside the women's restroom. On top of the clothing is a name badge. Stan picks it up, showing it to the detective.

"Firenza. The janitor who walked out of the closet." Fox spins, checking around the space. The rest area is eerily still.

"Walked out of the closet?" Stan tightens and backs to the wall. "What are we doing?"

"I need to check the closet." The detective pulls the door open. The young janitor sits in the corner of the tiny room, gazing in a mirror at the two-carat diamond earrings dazzling her earlobes.

"We have to go back to Jupiter. I've failed quite miserably and I don't understand how. We've got to find Dalia."

twenty
mixing metaphors in the art of war

"JUPITER? Dr. Argall, you owe me an explanation." Stan Baskins blocks the door to the car. "What happened in the restroom?"

The detective shakes his head. "This is the crux. I had the checkmate in four moves, and my opponent's playing on another board." His eyes are on his phone, flipping it backward and forward.

Stan moves into Fox's space. "No, my friend. No meltdowns into your personal rabbit holes. Plus, you're mixing metaphors. And violating an important Art of War. Never mistake Intersecting Highways for Dispersive Ground."

"Sun Tzu, The Nine Situations. Yes, yes. I made an assumption we were on our own territory in this fight. A failed point of view."

"And when you find yourself on Intersecting Highways, you are to join hands with your allies. I'm your ally. We'll sit, and you'll walk through this with me. I'm warning you. You may be a better chess player, but I'm awesome at puzzles and I always notice a blank space. Sit in the car and start a new game of Brick Breaker. And talk."

Stan opens the passenger door and waves Fox in while

reviewing the parking lot. The rest area traffic has normalized. Going to his door, he says, "OK, tell me the story."

"Evidence—clearly planted—brings Tick into the frame of a suspicious death. I say 'planted' based on fact, not emotion. I'll sort it for you, first things first. In chronology, but please interrupt me if I lose you."

"I promise I will."

"I found an odd piece of sweater-like knitted material at the Martin county sheriff's department. At a county task force delegation meeting. Cap insists I attend these. I'm certain they're valuable, but my attendance? Surely a waste."

Fox knocks a ball into the electronic wall, blasting the rest of the bricks.

"Surely a waste, indeed. You're quite efficient in your game."

"Well, hello. The knitted material had a small clump of vomitus containing coffee ground blood. And quite a tiny spot with an odor of methamphetamine. I know, a little hard to understand, but I process odors differently. Should I explain?"

"Please."

"Odors trigger varying neural activity, but in me, the elicitation is in the posteromedial cortex — bear with me a minute — which is an integrated hub in the brain. You have a posteromedial cortex, true, but I'm afraid you almost certainly use only a single region called the piriform cortex for olfactory matters. This limits your ability to recognize and find useful information in odors. Sorry, but there it is." Fox hasn't started a new game, but he stares at the phone.

"I think I'll survive the disappointment."

"You're proficient at other things, as you have mentioned. Puzzles. Very important for your job at the FBI."

"Exactly. Now, let's accept the meth and blood evidence as

presented. Charlie Perez confirmed the forensics information you've summarized?"

"Yes. I found the initial piece of material at a task force meeting in Stuart. A day and a half later, we were called to a scene on the Jupiter Inlet Light. Odd, because the Lighthouse was closed at the time. The remainder of the sweater was lashed to the top railing, saturated with fresh blood, which dripped onto the concrete. A human top lip was strung over the knitted material." Fox's gaze moves to the window. "Charlie asked me to consider — she said 'ponder' — the temperature issues. Temperature and specimen condition."

"And? Have you pondered?"

"Oh, crikey." He slams his head on the headrest. "I've got what I missed, at least."

"Sharing is caring."

"The blood wasn't in the same condition as the excised lip. The blood was fresh, and the lip was excised perimortem. Around the time of the death."

"So, at least a day and a half delta between the lip and the blood, based on finding the first knit at the Martin county sheriff's. 'Peri'. Is that Latin?"

"Greek. 'Mortem' is Latin." Fox stops and puts his phone down. "Weird we put them together. I wouldn't have, of course. Not much blood in the lip excision, although we had some indication the injury was not post-mortem. So, the blood soaking the sweater and spilling onto the concrete had to be refrigerated. Not a difficult leap, but getting it all to come together would be a challenge."

"Is something coming together for you?"

"It's beginning to make more sense. A woman from The Colony reported the sweater on the railing while star-gazing with binoculars. The story appears plausible, but she also called the cop I met at the scene 'Guy.' She said 'Guy came right over.' At the time, I thought she generically referred to

The Sweater Case

him as a 'guy.' What if she didn't? I need to find out his name."

"We need to interview her again and pull him in?"

"We?" Fox cocks his head at his colleague. "You'll have to manage Cap to enter any interview room in Palm Beach."

"Half my job is to get in other people's interview rooms. Leave it to me. Now. If you think I'm distracted from your trip to the Women's toilets, I'm not. Continue and make sure you explain the 'woman' you asked about."

"Well, umm, the text came from a woman I met in Boston, where I practiced law. She's also a lawyer. She... Umm, she takes an avid interest in me."

"Avid interest?"

"Special." The detective squirms in his seat and picks up his phone. "Intense."

"And?"

"She told me the meth trail is real, but not as pertinent to the murder as I assumed. I take her comment to mean my murderer or murderers are not limited to the Detroit or Gwinnett drug machines."

"So your Stalker Woman knew we were on the turnpike heading north and where we were in our drive? And she has information about the murder and sweater evidence? Does the fact she tracks your activity bother you? Because it bothers me."

"Oh, without a doubt, but I already know how she gleaned the turnpike knowledge. A lucky break for her, I suspect. I'm sure she got quite the kick." Fox is relaxed again, fingers flying on his device.

"You're going to explain?"

"This weekend I lost my wife for a few minutes. The door to the garage, as well as her passenger car door, was standing open. I found Grace in the alley. I'll be shocked if she doesn't have a listening device on her phone. I spoke to her when we left and told her we were going turnpike."

"Extremely creepy. Your old colleague is in deep trouble."

"If you can catch her doing it," Fox says with a grim smile. "Good luck. The knowledge about the murder and evidence? Significantly more disturbing, and still a mystery to me. Natalie won't leave an open trail. She's a sociopath."

"Lovely."

Fox's phone rings. "Argall. His face drains of color.

"What?"

"Marley and her family, Theiss, Josh. They had an accident on I-95 at the Palm Beach Airport exit. I need to go home. Now."

twenty-one
making good choices

ROOFIE GLANCES in his rear-view mirror. "Blue lights, Tick. We're getting pulled over."

"It'll be nothing. You weren't speeding." Tick rests his head against the seat, his eyes closed.

"No, I wasn't. And since when do sheriff cars pull Floridians over for speeding on the interstate? State patrols don't even stop speeders here."

Tick's eyes fly open, and he turns. "A Palm Beach sheriff. We're still in St. Lucie county."

"Tick, settle yourself now. This may be Cap sending a car."

"For me." A flush fills his face, his pain palpable.

"Yes. Rest, son. Trust Cap and Fox. I do." Roofie veers the car to the side of the road.

The sheriff's vehicle pulls behind, and a young deputy approaches the passenger window and salutes.

"Sergeant John Tickman? We're going to need to take you the rest of the way. Captain Harley sent us to escort you to the sheriff's department in Palm Beach." The man shifts his feet, looking down.

A second deputy stands in front of the cruiser. *What do they think I'm going to do? What were they told?*

"No problem, Deputy," Tick says. "Mind if I bring my overnight bag? Just coming back from vacation."

"I'm sorry, sir. You'll have to come with us." The deputy steps away from the passenger door and takes a wide-legged stance.

Smiling, Tick raises his hands, showing his palms. "No problem, Deputy. Guess my chronic tardiness finally pissed Cap off."

The man doesn't move or return the smile.

Tick exits the car, keeping his palms up as he waves to the second deputy. "Artie. Glad to see you. How's the kid doing in boot camp?"

"Not much news, Sergeant, but she appreciated your talk with her." Artie shuffles, looking away at the rushing traffic on the road.

"With her brain, she'll be running PsyOps soon."

"Thanks, Sarge."

Once Tick clears Roofie's car, the second deputy walks him to the back of the sheriff's vehicle, opening the door for him. "Thanks, Sarge," he says again.

"I grew up rough in Riviera Beach and this is the first time I've been in the back of a law enforcement vehicle."

Roofie listens to Tick speak to the deputy, and the deep sadness in the sergeant's voice breaks his heart. The minister meets eyes with the first deputy, who remains in the same spot outside the passenger door. "Do you need anything more from me, Deputy?"

The young man shakes his head, murmuring, "We respect John Tickman, sir. He's a hero to us. I promise to watch out for him."

"You do that, friend. He's one to emulate."

The Sweater Case

"I'm dropping you at the ER, Fox. I'm sure Grace is already in the hospital." Stan pulls into the main entrance to St. Mary's Medical Center in Palm Beach.

"Grace isn't answering my calls. She's not at work. I've spoken to Stella and Beth and they haven't spoken to my wife."

"If she's here, it could be an issue with her phone in the hospital. Go in. I'll be right over."

The detective doesn't move.

"Fox, go in."

"Where is Grace? Beth, Stella, her best friends; they're our family. They can't find her. No one knows where my wife is."

Stan puts the car in park in front of the emergency room doors. "Come on, Dr. Argall. I'll walk you in. Let's go."

"I need to call her once more." Fox dials the phone, and again, no answer. He slumps in the seat.

"Fox..." Stan starts, as a woman in a nurse's uniform stalks out of the ER.

"Ellis, stand up," the woman orders. "We're going into the Emergency Room. Roofie's meeting us here. He's about ten minutes away. Come, sweetie. Theiss is OK, our babies are OK, but Marley needs you."

"Stel, where's Grace?"

"Yes, honey, we're looking for her. You must come in and focus on Marley. Grace would want you to focus on your daughter. Beth is with her. Come, and be your best self, Ellis. Make good choices." Stel leans into the window and stares down Stan. "Are you leaving this car here, blocking this area?"

"No, ma'am. I'm about to move it."

"Do it now. Ellis, come." Stella takes the detective's arm and walks him forward. "Am I going to regret this?"

"No, no. I'm here. I need my phone." Fox shivers. "Give me a minute. I'm here. I'm staying with you."

"Yes. Stay with us for Marley and Theiss."

As the automatic doors slide open, the detective says, "I'm sorry, Stel. I'll need you to keep me focused. Grace is missing, and I can't pretend otherwise."

twenty-two
anchors, away

AS STAN ENTERS THE ER, a balding man greets him.
"Are you the officer who brought Ellis Argall here?" The man asks. "I'm Jacob Moreno. I work with Roofie Parks."
"I'm Stan Baskins. I work with Ellis... Fox. The lady I met outside mentioned Roofie, but I haven't met him. Or the lady."
"She would be Stella, Roofie's wife. They're long-time friends of the Argalls. May I call you Stan? Without Grace, Roofie may be the only one who can manage this situation. The Parks and Argalls have been together since college at Ohio State. Would you sit with me, while we wait for Roofie?" Jacob leads the FBI agent to a separate grouping of hard plastic chairs. "Ellis' son-in-law was killed in the accident. Marley's OK, as is Theiss. Theiss is still being checked, but the doctors say there are no genuine concerns. I'm a pastor who serves this hospital, and I'm assured by staff the girls only suffered some bruises and scratches."
"What happened?"
"A driver was drinking. He hit them broadside as he tried to merge from the Palm Beach International Airport exit

ramp. The one going north. He hit Josh's door, the driver's door, almost head-on. Josh died instantly. The car spun, but it whirled to a stop. The surrounding drivers were able to avoid the accident, so no pile-up. The girls were shaken, but not seriously injured."

The hospital doors swish open, and a middle-aged man hurries in, looking around. He spots Jacob.

"Roofie." Jacob stands to hug him, holding him for a long time.

Jacob talks softly, and Stan realizes he's praying. The men pray together out loud in a back-and-forth way the federal agent has never seen before. When they break apart, Roofie reaches his hand out to Stan.

"You must be Stan, the FBI agent. Ellis speaks of you often, and finds you 'interesting.' Quite the compliment." Roofie pats the agent on the shoulder. "We'll be in some intense moments, Stan. Can I ask you a favor?"

He's going to ask me to leave.

"Will you go back with us, and tell Ellis you'll personally go find Grace? It'll give him some relief. He respects you."

"Sure, but maybe Tick...?" Stan starts.

"Tick's been taken in for questioning in the recent case. He'll not be available for a while." The pastor waits for Stan's reaction, assessing. "I can help Marley and Theiss, and Grace when we find her. You could help Ellis. He'll be crushed, losing multiple anchors in his life at once. You may not know Ellis is on the autism spectrum. He relies on certain people to support him."

"My first cousin, Max, is autistic. I grew up with him, in the same home. He's an astrophysicist at NASA. I get the assignment."

"Sounds perfect, let's go."

Jacob drops into one of the plastic chairs. "I'll stay here and wait for Grace."

Roofie and Stan head to the desk, and the clerk greets them. "Reverend Parks, the family is in Room One, the first glassed room on the right. I'll buzz you in."

The double doors swish into the treatment area. A windowed room is in front of them, the curtains drawn. Stan holds the door open for Roofie to enter. An exceptionally tall woman kneels in front of a female version of Fox.

She must be Marley.

The detective crouches in the corner beside his daughter's chair. Marley's face is a mask, and she's covered in blood.

Fox's gaze flicks up and meets the agent's, before skittering away.

He's panicking.

"Roof." The tall woman moves aside for the pastor. Fox, Marley, and Roofie fall together in a group hug.

"I'm Marley's Aunt Beth." The woman sticks her hand out to Stan. "I'll be Dr. Wilson to you."

"Dr. Wilson." Stan drops his eyes to avoid reacting to the rude comment and answers quietly, "I'm Stan Baskins, an FBI agent working with Fox. Reverend Parks suggested I tell you all I'm leaving to find Mrs. Argall."

"*Doctor* Argall. Dr. Grace Argall." Beth Wilson glares at Stan.

"Aunt Beth," Marley says calmly. "Agent Baskins is our friend."

Beth harrumphs, not backing down.

Marley pulls herself up from the chair and crosses the room. "I'm grateful, Agent Baskins, as is my father and my Aunt Beth."

"No problem." *She's so much like him.*

"My Dad speaks highly of you. That's interesting." Marley leans on Beth Wilson's shoulder and manages a weak smile.

"So I heard," Stan murmurs. "I'm leaving, but I'll keep in

touch. I don't have the words to say how sorry I am, Marley. To you all."

"Thank you, Stan. Please find my mother."

twenty-three
define 'insane'

"WAIT, Agent Baskins. May I make a request?" Marley turns to her dad, who's talking with Roofie. "Dad? Would you mind going to help find Mom? We're aware we have a problem. Pretending won't help me or Theiss."

"Marls..." Fox shakes his head and shivers.

"*Fel sy'n addas. I mi, Dadi.*" [As is suitable. For me, Daddy.]

"*Mae rhannau ohonof i ar goll, fy merch.*" [Parts of me are missing, my daughter.] Tears drip from his face. "I'm lost."

Marley hugs him tight. "My hero is never lost, Daddy. You're the one Mom needs. And *I* need Mom."

"You go," Roofie agrees. "We're all here, El. Beth, Stel, me. We're with Marls and Theiss. Do your thing."

"I need to think." Fox fumbles with his phone and sways in an odd dance.

Her arm clutching her dad's waist, Marley walks him to the doors. "I'll tell Theissey Papa went for Nana."

Fox leans toward the FBI agent as the men walk from the room and says quietly, "Let's make this quick, Stan. I need to get to Tick soon. Cap talked about sending a car for him.

Roofie wouldn't tell me if they've picked up Tick; he's protective. But my partner would be here right now if he was free."

"I'm sure he would be, Fox." *'Quick?' He's focused on Tick and not Grace? What have I got here?*

"I'll bet you a bottle of Blanton's we can find Gracie right now. We need to do this carefully, or my actions will blow up in my face."

"In *our* faces, Lieutenant. I'm backing your play unless it's insane. Then I'm handcuffing you to my car and calling Cap."

"Define 'insane'." Fox opens the driver's door to Stan's car and gets in. "We go to my house. I'll drive."

"And explain." Hesitating, the agent says, "I'm very sorry about your son-in-law."

"Yes. Well, everything will sink in when we have Tick and my Gracie back. Josh was a wonderful husband to Marley. And a perfect father to Theiss." Fox pulls onto Military Trail and heads to Abacoa. "Grace and I had an odd interaction last weekend."

"The listening device in her phone?"

"Yes. We don't do coincidences, do we?"

"Not usually."

"This is connected to the spying device. Probably. I just don't know. How are you with a gun?"

"Other than I'm a cop?" Stan grimaces. "I'm a Marine, Fox. Train hard and never point a gun at something you don't plan to destroy."

"We may have a conflict with another law enforcement officer. How would you feel?"

"If the cop is dirty, I'm damned good about it."

Fox pulls into his driveway and opens the garage. His face twitches. "Grace's car is here."

"She's here? She's not answering anyone. Is she injured?"

"She's not here. Let's check the house, but my Gracie is

not here." Fox unlocks the door to the kitchen. "The home security is turned off."

He motions Stan to the bedroom on the first floor and heads upstairs, his weapon out.

Minutes later, Fox comes down the stairs to find Stan in the living room. "Upstairs is clear."

"Clear here, but a struggle took place in your master."

"I would hope so. I wouldn't want her to go easily." Fox examines the wrecked bedroom. Bedclothes are on the floor, and drawers are emptied into scattered piles. "Rather than a search for anything, the disarray is more like a tantrum."

Stan points to the bathroom. "Easy, Fox, but we have a crime scene with injury in here."

"In the left sink?"

Turning to the detective, Stan blinks. "How did you know?"

Fox assesses the blood pooled in the fixture and chuckles. "My sweet, sweet Gracie. It must have been difficult for you."

"Come look at this." Stan points to a tiny scrawl on Grace's make-up table. "RHYBUDD. Mean anything to you?'

"Yup. I'm betting '*rhybuddio.*' 'Warn' in Welsh. My girl."

"You and Marley were speaking Welsh? More importantly, why are you so relaxed about this blood?" Stan scowls. "We have a problem here."

Fox waves the FBI agent into the bathroom and points to the sink. "See this blood? The mucus? The blood is from a nosebleed. I'm not relaxed, I'm focused. Gracie and I have a safety plan in place. We've role-played it many times. If someone enters the house, head straight to the bathroom. This room has a triple lock, and the door is protected against gunfire. Pepper spray in the cabinet over the left sink. Fight as a last resort; aim for the genitals or nose."

"Your wife clocked the bad guy."

"It would appear so. I'm concerned, of course, I am. This

may be Natalie Forester's work, and if she's involved, I'm praying she would never permit any real harm to Grace. Her game would end forever if she baited me by hurting my wife. My bet is she enjoys her fun too much. Yes, Welsh. I came to university in Columbus, Ohio, met my Gracie, and never left. In truth, I always knew my life would play out here and not in my dear Wales."

"So where is Grace? How long ago did this assault occur?"

The detective leans over and sniffs the blood. "As expected, the blood is coagulated but not completely dry. Any blood in this sink with the mucus would dry more slowly. Note the A/C is way down. To freezing, I'm telling you. I suffer. This gore is from a nosebleed, and I'm certain Gracie dealt her assailant a blow. Less than an hour, I'd wager. I'm convinced this is the perp's blood."

"Or Grace's, Fox. We have to find her."

twenty-four
finding grace

"THE SMALL AMOUNT of blood in the sink is the only blood in the room. Unlikely to have been so neatly done, if the blood were Gracie's from an attack. No, it's the assailant's blood. My wife defended herself. Now, for the complication. I think the assailant is a Martin county deputy sheriff named Ann Carley."

Stan spins to stare at Fox. "Why the hell would you think that?"

"Because I believe she ran interference while Natalie messed with Gracie's phone. I'll explain, eventually. First, we must recover my wife. Are you in? To be clear, I don't advise you to try to stop me. I'm stronger than I appear and quite adept at controlling my physical environment. I don't want to hurt you, but I will."

"At the right time, we'll test your confidence, but not today." Stan smiles at the older man. "I'm in. We have kidnapping and a meth connection, correct? Federal crimes. Where are we going?"

"Two houses down. You go to the front, and I'll go to the back."

"Two houses down?" Stan says, stunned. "What's going on here?"

"I truly don't understand it all yet. Let's go talk to Ann Carley and find out."

Fox heads out of the kitchen to the fenced backyard. He stands against the high fence by the gate to the alley, waving Stan over.

"The house is on this side of the alley — the yellow one with the black shutters. Avoid the front window, and knock on the front door. I'm sure the deputy will be home, and she'll be alone. Natalie will expect me to show up and will leave Ann exposed. In fact, it's what she wants. Ann's a sacrifice."

"Natalie won't be at the house?"

Fox laughs bitterly. "Oh, no. Natalie Forester's on a private plane somewhere, winging away."

The two men go through the gate and split up, with the detective heading down the alley along the back fences.

Stan walks up the concrete path to the yellow house. He rings the doorbell and hears it trill inside.

Minutes pass. Stan tries the handle. *Locked.*

"Can I help you?" A woman stands at the corner of the closed garage. She's wearing a sheriff's uniform, her gun holstered. Her nose appears broken.

"I'm meeting a friend here. I think this is the right house." Stan grins and starts toward the Deputy. "Stan Baskins. I'm meeting Ellis. Wow, I'm sorry about your injury. I've had a broken nose. Totally not fun."

"No Ellis here, Stan. You should check the address."

Ann turns and finds Fox behind her.

"Dr. Argall. How can I help you? Ah, that's right. 'Ellis.' How can I help you, gentlemen?"

"Ann, my wife Grace is missing. I hoped to get your help to find her."

"I haven't seen her. Sorry, I'm on my way to work."

"Stan and I found a bit of a mess at my house. I don't want to impact what could be a crime scene. I've called it in but would love to discuss it with you. I admit I'm a bit worried."

"I'd love to, of course, but I'm afraid I must head to work." Ann shifts to allow a view of both men. "And exactly who is your friend Stan?"

"I can call the sheriff." Fox waves the deputy to the front door. "I'm sure he'll be fine with you helping a fellow LEO. I'm also a physician. I think I should examine your nose. It appears badly broken, and the swelling is significant."

Ann stares at Fox and Stan, hesitating. "Thanks, my nose is fine. Certainly, though, anything for a neighbor. I can be late to work. I'll make coffee."

Fox motions to the upstairs of the house as the men follow her in. Stan nods.

Settling in the kitchen, Ann fusses with the coffee maker, her back to the men. "I'm not sure how I can help. Maybe we can talk through the facts as you know them?"

"Sounds good," Fox says. "Grace hasn't answered her phone. I've told her forever to use the 'Find My Phone' thing, so I can spot her location."

"I think that's another function, Fox." Stan hovers by the door. "Deputy? I'd love a bathroom. Mind if I use yours?"

Ann stiffens almost imperceptibly and drops her arms to her side. "Sure. By the front door, a powder room. By the stairs." She watches as Stan leaves the kitchen, flexing her fists.

"To continue, our home alarm system was turned off, which may be a Gracie thing." Fox cocks his head to the side, watching Ann. "The real issue is in the master. The room is wrecked. But what concerns me, naff, really... I found clotted blood in the sink."

"Clotted blood? '*Naff*?'"

"'Naff, messy, yucky. Not a medical term." Fox smiles. "Coagulated blood and mucus. Quite a bit."

"Ann!" Stan calls as he walks back in. "Hey, something weird. This phone was in the bottom of your trash can. Didn't want you to lose it. It has a pretty red lion on it."

Fox moves to block the door to the exit. "Red lion? Nah, I believe that's a dragon. A Welsh Dragon. My Gracie's phone."

Ann starts to draw her gun, but Stan is first.

"Don't do it, Deputy." The FBI agent levels his weapon. "You've got way too much trouble in your life already."

"Where is my wife, Ann? Where's Grace?"

twenty-five
smelly letters, part deux?

"YOUR DNA IS on the ribbon, John." Cap leans back against the two-way mirror in Interview Room A. "The outdated license is not problematic, in my mind. To be honest, it proved the frame to me. Amateurish. Nevertheless, your DNA was discovered at a crime scene connected to your friend."

"Is anyone looking for Dalia? I mean, as opposed to hauling me in, wasting precious time?" Tick sits back in the chair, his arms crossed.

"Answer my questions and we'll get to the next steps faster."

"Thanks for not handcuffing me in a perp walk," the sergeant sneers.

Cap slings his arm over Tick's shoulders, lowering into his subordinate's face. "You saying you wouldn't be following up if the evidence was on me and not you?"

"I absolutely would be looking at you."

"Bravo. And you should be. I hope I taught you that much." The senior officer stretches his arms over his head, preening. "Have I ever told you I see you in my role, running the entire department?"

Tick's face reddens, and he stammers, "Uh... No, I never considered..."

"Well, I do. Tyler, let's start." Cap motions to roll the tape. "We're beginning our interview of Sergeant John Tickman, a detective on my staff at the Palm Beach county sheriff's violent crimes department. I'm Captain Skip Harley. Sergeant Tickman, are you aware we're taping this interview?"

"Yes."

"Were you informed your DNA is at a crime scene at the Jupiter Lighthouse? Please answer out loud, if you would."

"Yes."

"Do you know where your DNA was discovered?"

"On a military campaign ribbon. I was a primary investigator on the Lighthouse scene, with Lieutenant Fox—Ellis Argall."

"Were you aware at the time this military ribbon was yours?"

"No. This was a standard issue campaign award. No way to identify the recipient at the time."

"When did you become aware of the evidence?" Cap leans against the gray mirror.

"Not until yesterday, while I was out of town. On vacation."

Cap grits his teeth and growls. "Who informed you of the evidence?"

"Lieutenant Argall, by telephone."

"Do you own a property at 11 Sunset Drive in Tequesta, Florida?"

Tick's head snaps up. "Yes."

"When were you last at your home? Have you been to any location where you kept your personal military awards since Dr. Argall informed you of the evidence?"

"No, have you been to my house?" Tick snaps. Glaring at

the mirrored wall, he says loudly, "What about you guys? Been breaking into any of your colleagues' homes lately?"

"Detective Tickman. Please focus on me. Did a Palm Beach county sheriff meet you in St. Lucie county before you returned to your home from your... Vacation?"

"Yes."

"Did you call anyone to go to any location and examine any property related to this case?"

"No, I haven't."

"Is a storage unit on your property?"

"Yes."

"You been to your storage unit in the last week?"

"I haven't been in our storage unit in the last six months or more. Probably since last Christmas. Note, this is a separate storage area in a public laundry room. It has wooden doors and a simple keyed lock."

"Did you ever put an extra lock on the storage unit?" Cap asks.

"No. Nothing in my unit except holiday decorations. Nothing of any value."

"Did you store military awards or documents — for example, your outdated license — in your storage unit?"

"No. I have personal items in my desk inside my home." Tick exhales. "Everyone leaves their apartments unlocked in my complex if they are at the pool or community building. It would be easy to get access."

"Are you willing to accompany me to your apartment and storage unit and allow me to examine your property without a warrant?"

"No. I'll accompany you to my storage unit, but not my apartment. Not before I speak with a union rep."

"Fair enough. Let's go." Cap waves Tick up and signals to the viewing room. "Leslie, you drive us to the sergeant's storage unit. Under no circumstances is anyone to inform Fox Argall of our movements. Dr. Argall is not in this."

Over the speaker, Leslie says, "Cap, we were informed a fatal car accident occurred 30 minutes ago near Palm Beach International Airport. The fatality was Lieutenant Argall's son-in-law."

Cap groans. "Josh? Anyone else in the car? Two-car accident? Details."

"Yes, a Joshua Clairmont was dead on scene. Two other passengers in the car, an adult female and a child. Both transported to St. Mary's. Other driver faulted, arrested for DUI. Somebody informed Lieutenant Argall, but we have no knowledge of his location at this time."

"How and where was Fox contacted?" Tick asks.

"By mobile. No info about his whereabouts," the deputy repeats.

"Cap, we need to get to the hospital." Tick heads for the door.

"No, we do *not*. Leslie, you'll drive Sergeant Tickman and me to Tequesta to examine the storage unit. Roger, you call Reverend Edgar Parks and tell him everything about this accident. Ask the Reverend to go to St. Mary's Hospital. Tick, we have our work. Roofie can handle the Argalls."

Forty minutes later, Cap, Tick, and Leslie pull into Tick's apartment complex.

"A shuffleboard court?" Cap says, pointing past the pool.

"Yes, we're big on shuffling here. One of my neighbors—a 91-year-old World War II vet—won our annual tournament this year, out of 27 entrants in the men's division. Pete has been the shuffleboard teacher here for years. He taught my mom. We all love the guy. He's the Activities Director." Tick rattles on, voice shaking.

"Uh, isn't this an over-55 community?" Cap pats his sergeant's shoulder. "How does my 32-year-old detective live here?"

"With his 56-year-old mom." Tick grins, then remembers why they're here. "I'm not going to upset her, man. No going into my place unless you force me. I'm innocent here, and you know it."

"Only the storage unit now, Ticker."

"We go up on this side, OK? I want to avoid Mom seeing us out the window." Tick leads the officers to the stairs and up to the second floor. "Right through here, past the laundry area. No one keeps anything in here of value, I can tell you. This is overflow for holiday decorations."

Tick stops at a slatted, wooden door halfway through the dark hall. As the door swings open, a waft of perfume hits them. "That sweet aroma. The same as the smelly letters from the Conway case. What is it?"

"Nina Ricci L'Air du Temps," Leslie answers. "I buy it for my Nan."

"I'm more interested in the chair," Cap points to the back of the unit.

A large object sits on a chair shoved in the corner of the storage unit, covered in a bright blue blanket.

"That's not my chair," Tick mutters. "I don't recognize the blanket."

"Stand back, and secure the area. Tick, you do not move. Leslie, tape this area off on the balcony, and no one leaves until I say so." Cap scrambles into gloves and footies, and drags the blanket down, dropping to his knees in front of the chair. "Oh, Grace. *Gracie.*"

twenty-six
come back to me, girl

TICK RUSHES into the storage unit, throwing himself on the floor beside the chair. "Gracie! Oh, God, please!" He folds his arms over his face, groaning.

"Move back! Move!" Cap yanks the young deputy backward. "Leslie, take him out!"

Grace's face is gray, her eyes rolled back in her head. Her lips are tinged with blue, spreading up around her nose.

Cap tugs the chair out one-handed, slamming into Tick. "You get your shit together and move out of this storage unit, Sergeant, or I'll kick your ass down those stairs."

He drags Grace's body onto the concrete hallway, dropping to administer Narcan nasal spray. "She has a pulse, seriously thready and weak. Call a bus right now, Deputy Youssef. Remove Sergeant Tickman. Now."

Leslie Youssef grabs her phone. "Sergeant, please. I can't physically carry you. Walk."

"I'm coming," Tick moans. "You don't understand, Leslie."

"I understand." She dials her phone. "This is Deputy Sheriff Leslie Youssef. I need an ambulance at — what's the address here?"

"Give it to me."

She shoves the phone into his hand.

Tears pour down his face as he says, "This is Sergeant John Tickman, Palm Beach sheriff. Send the bus to 11 Sunset, Tequesta. You're a half mile from here, off Seacrest. We'll meet you out front to show you in." Stumbling to his feet, he heads out the door, wiping his eyes.

"Deputy Youssef, you accompany Sergeant Tickman every step he takes, got it? Every fucking step." Cap leans down and checks Grace's breathing as the two officers leave the unit and disappear. "Gracie, oh, Gracie. What will any of us do? Come back, *arhoswch yma, merch. Arhoswch yma gyda mi.*" [Come back to me, girl. Stay with me.]

⸻

As the ambulance drives away with Grace, Cap glares at his officers. "Deputy Youssef, drive Sergeant Tickman back to the department. Tick, you're not free to go to the hospital, to any hospital with a single damn Argall. Nor are you free to talk to Fox. Not free. I'll call Roofie myself. You stay out of everything. Do you hear me?"

Tick stares off, his jaw tense. Leslie Youssef punches her colleague's arm and walks to their car.

"I'm protecting my staff, Tick." Cap pokes the sergeant in his tie. "You're my responsibility. I'll have your agreement right now to trust me. If you think you can pick up bad habits from your partner, I'm clearly warning you. Do not push me on this."

"Sergeant? Come on," Leslie calls.

His fists clenched, Tick mumbles, "I know. I do know."

"Then git. Buy a fancy coffee. I'll finish up here. Wait in my office. Inside my office, with the door closed." Cap shoos his subordinate away. "And don't touch my orchids."

After his team leaves, he leans his head against the stair railing.

"My boy respects you, Captain. He'll do as you say."

He turns to the voice; a woman standing on the upper balcony. "Mrs. Tickman?"

"Blanche."

"Blanche, I love your boy."

"Yes, you do, Captain. He knows it, too. You'll call me if he gets into any real trouble, won't you?"

"It's not Tick who worries me, Blanche. Not even Dr. Argall. Well, maybe Dr. Argall."

"I pray for you every day."

"We all need it. Glad to meet you, ma'am." Cap nods to Blanche and starts walking. As he clears the apartment complex, he dials Roofie Parks.

"Roofie, this is Skip Harley. We found Grace Argall; she's in bad shape. Appears it's a heroin overdose with a head injury. Transport to Jupiter Medical Center."

"Narcan?" Roofie murmurs, his voice far away.

"Yes, but not without a delay. We won't understand much until she's examined. How is Marley?"

"Marley was trained from birth to under-react, as I'm sure you can imagine. She's holding up right now, but she's still in shock. She and Theiss are fine physically. The drunk driver took Josh on an angle, and the car spun. Luckily, other drivers witnessed the accident and were able to stop."

"Where's Fox?"

"I'm not sure. He's with Stan, the FBI agent." Roofie's voice cracks. "Stan appears able to handle our Ellis. They left the hospital to look for Grace."

"I'll pick up Fox. I've ordered him brought to the hospital." Cap sighs. "Are you able to... support Marley in all this?"

"I don't think Marley is our problem, Skip."

"No, Roofie, she's not."

The silence is thick.

"Thanks, Reverend." The captain ends the call and takes off walking. His phone sings Pachelbel's Canon in D, the ring for Missy, his executive administrative assistant.

"Lieutenant Argall just called in two crime scenes, one at his home, and the second at a neighbor's. He called for backup and wanted me to tell you personally he's holding Deputy Ann Carley for transport and questioning."

"Fuck. Aww, I'm sorry, Miss, listen, I'm running out of people who can handle the good doctor. Tick..."

"Sergeant Tickman is on his way in. Deputy Youssef called. I'll keep him from Dr. Argall."

"I'm going to walk a few minutes and think this over. Send a car for me at the bridge on Highway One, Jupiter side, would ya?" Cap hesitates. "Listen, Missy. Tick is to stay in my office. You and Youssef guard him. If he tries to leave, you have my permission to use your martial arts training."

Missy chuckles. "He's six foot six, Cap. I'll need a tranq gun."

"I'm going to send a Jupiter Police car for Fox, but if I miss him... If Dr. Argall shows up at the department, have him escorted to the IT room off Interview C."

"I'll shut him in with Tyler, they like each other," Missy agrees. "Deputy at the door. I won't let him see Sergeant Tickman."

Cap grinds his teeth. "Escort Ann Carley to Interview C. No one gets access to her until I speak to her supervisor. No one. If Fox throws a fit, I want him restrained and put in lock-up. I mean it, Miss, cuff him and lock him up."

twenty-seven
pipe dreams

"I'M SORRY, LIEUTENANT," the Jupiter Police officer says. "Captain Harley gave detailed instructions to take you to him immediately."

"Gladys, I must accompany Ann Carley to the sheriff's department. This woman's a critical witness in a homicide, if not the prime suspect." Fox blinks rapidly. "Cap isn't aware of the import..."

"I think your captain is fully informed, Lieutenant Argall. Order from my boss. We've known each other for fifteen years. Have I ever been anything less than collegial to you as you tromp through my patch?"

"No, of course not, Gladys." Fox tries to smile, but can't. "I'm conflicted."

"Come, Dr. Argall. Let's go," Gladys pats his arm. "Charlie Perez is on her way here. Your guys will take the deputy into your department. Your colleagues are also law enforcement professionals. They can handle the scenes."

"Stan?" Fox turns to the FBI agent.

"I'll go in with the Palm Beach deputies. You go to Cap."

"Stan, someone needs to be here to search Carley's house."

"We searched. South Florida, no basement. We checked the attic space. Charlie Perez is coming."

"She'll want to go to my house first."

"Let Charlie do her job, Fox. If you want to advise her to start at Carley's house, text her. But let her decide." Stan walks the detective to the cruiser. "Call me when you can talk."

"I've got to go in and interview the deputy."

"Captain Harley will never let you interview Carley. That'll be a frickin' mess. Think about it. What would you do in his shoes?"

"OK, alright," Fox sighs. "Gladys. Deliver me to Captain Harley. Where is he, anyway?"

"He's at the Jupiter Medical Center."

"Ah." Fox drops his head and he stammers, "The fog clears. My Gracie."

⸻

Cap and Roofie stand outside the ER as the cruiser pulls up.

Fox opens the door of the car wearily, not getting out. "What happened? Is it Grace?"

Roofie and Cap surround him, and the pastor puts his hand out to his friend.

"El, she's stable. Someone hurt Grace, but she's stable. Stable."

"What happened? Where is she?"

"We're going in," Cap says, softly. "Grace is in the ER, and Marley's already here."

Marley is standing in the hallway outside a room. "Mom's stable, Dad. She's breathing normally and everything is coming back in line. Say nothing about... Don't mention my... Josh. We haven't told her about the accident."

Fox walks to the door and stops. Grace is talking to a

physician. She looks up at her husband and smiles. The detective jerks and stiffens.

Marley whispers, "Mom was overdosed, Dad. Heroin. She suffered a head injury."

"Lad, come here. I'm fine. Come, hold me." Grace smiles. "I'm OK."

He shuffles in his dance and bursts into tears, covering his face with his hands.

"Come here, Lad. Help your dad, Marls."

"We need to re-interview Alexi Gardarov." Cap's leaning back in a plastic hospital chair in the light green hallway outside Grace's room, trying to assess the case.

Fox stands ramrod against the doorframe to Gracie's room playing Brick Breaker, his jaw muscle flexing. He ignores the captain.

"You listening? I need you for the Gardarov interview, Lieutenant. We still haven't found Dalia. Are you able?"

"Of course I'm able," the detective murmurs, not looking up. "You saved my Gracie's life."

"I did my job, but I can't be more grateful for the opportunity to find her in time."

"I'm best used to interview Ann Carley."

"Can't happen, Counselor. I'm not having a ridiculous debate about it."

"Alright, I'm in the IT room as you and Stan interview her. I feed you questions." Fox turns to Grace's room. "Narcan might make her sick."

Cap stares at his detective. "Why'd you let me win so quick?"

Fox shrugs. "I've a temper at times. Only when I'm pressed, but there it is. Her answers may upset me. While being angry may work better in certain interviews, Ann's a victim of a sort. My anger may not be useful. Ann Carley can tell us where Dalia is being held."

"You believe Dalia is still alive? Fox, that's a pipe dream."

"She's alive." Fox walks into his wife's room. "Gracie, I have a few questions, then I must go find Dalia."

Grace sits on the side of the ER bed talking with Marley and Roofie. "Of course, you do, Lad. I'm fine, just nauseated. Surrounded by fussing friends and family. Stel's on her way down. Beth's coming. Ask your questions." She rubs her stomach and grimaces.

"You'll be better at home, my girl. They'll release you soon. Marley, are you and Theiss staying with us? I suggest it's best."

Cap walks into the room from the hall. "I've assigned two cars to your house, Fox. One in the alley and one out front."

"My family's safe now that we have Ann Carley in custody. This thing with Gracie is a one-off. I don't believe it was part of any plan. Ann has much bigger issues than the Argalls."

"We don't understand her involvement in any of this, Fox," Cap objects. "How will it play out?"

"How's Ann Carley involved, Gracie?" Fox hugs his wife, kissing her hair.

"The person I smashed in the face was wearing a balaclava and hoodie. They were about Marley's height and weighed a good 30 pounds more than her. I got one lick in before lights out."

"A wonderful hit. You made me proud, girlie. And the abbreviated 'Warn.' You remembered your Welsh. It all led me in the right direction. *Fy ngwraig wych.*" [My wonderful wife.]

"Did the person have a sweet aroma?" Cap asks.

"An aroma?" Fox turns to his boss. "What an odd question from you. You can't even smell those orchids. The odors are all jumbled: mixed, sweet, spicy, citrus. Together, they're atrocious. They're as nauseating as Narcan."

"Just a question."

"No, it's not. Grace? Any sweet odor?"

"I can't recall any odor."

Cap motions for Fox to follow him. "I'm so glad you're OK, Gracie. I must take your husband."

twenty-eight
rich people are different

CAP AND FOX walk into the office of the chief of police for the Jupiter Inlet Colony. Jamie Watters appears miniature behind an enormous ornate mahogany desk rising off an expensive hand-loomed rug on carved legs. Original art hangs on the walls above antique tables and chairs.

"Come in, Skip! Good to see you again. It's been a while."

"*Trés* plush, Jamie. You've come quite a way from our Riviera Beach beat."

"My voters have expectations." Jamie Watters grins. "Suited for the chief of police in the exclusive Jupiter Inlet Colony. Not nearly as hard on my feet."

"I'll bet. Listen, Jamie. My lieutenant and I need to interview Representative Harris and his—whatever he is—valet servant Alexi Gardarov. I wanted to give you the courtesy."

"Well, Skip, I'm appreciative you understand my need to protect my people. I'd like one of my officers to ride along. Rich people are different. Rich and famous? Different again. Rich from 'serving' in politics, that's a new level of difference." Chief Watters leans back but keeps his eyes on Fox, who has slung himself into a chair near the door.

"Of course, your team was with us for the first interview.

Alexi Gardarov is a valet or something?" Cap tries to maintain eye contact with the chief while watching his detective.

"Ah, I dunno, Skip. A butler?" Watters calls up something on his computer. "He's concealed carry. Ex-Marine, quiet."

"Really?" Fox mutters, his head still in his game. "I thought he was quite talkative in our interview."

"Uh... Well, let me gander at the notes." Watters' West Virginia accent deepens as he taps on his computer with two fingers. "Got the verbatim here. He literally said twenty-two words in over an hour."

Fox stands from his chair and walks to the police chief. "Yes, but read the twenty-two words. If I remember correctly, he said: 'Michael Harris isn't home, and isn't expected home for several weeks. A conversation with the congressman offers no light on your investigation.'"

"Um, yes, that's right, Dr. Argall."

"When, in fact, Representative Harris was in his office, not fifty feet away, according to the interview he gave on a national news station the same day." Fox sits on the edge of Watters' desk.

"Now, I doubt..."

"The view behind him, out the window, was definitely your patch, Chief. I suspect the wall hangings will confirm where the interview took place."

Cap leans forward, elbows on knees, but doesn't speak.

"Well, Dr. Argall, I have no independent knowledge of the interview. I'm sure his staff wasn't aware of his location."

"Except they were," Fox murmurs.

"We'll need to interview all the people at the house, Jamie, and the houses surrounding." Cap's tone brooks no argument.

"I'm sure the congressman will be glad to make himself available, boys. You'll understand his schedule..."

The Sweater Case

"This is a murder, Jamie," Cap says. "You aren't running interference, are you?"

"No, Skip, I'm not. I don't like..."

Fox leans into his accent and smiles brightly. "Let's not worry about liking legitimate questions, Chief Watters. They're often quite unlikeable, in my experience."

Cap stands up, joining his detective in front of the Chief's mahogany desk. "Dr. Argall will be respectful of the congressman. I suggest he would rather interview here, in his home, than interview in DC. You're on his re-election committee, aren't you? What would you recommend to him? As the best location for our talk?"

"We simply need his help. For a constituent. A vulnerable person, as it happens," Fox agrees. "Is the congressman home in Florida this weekend? Important elections are around the corner."

Nausea floods Watters' face, and he can't hide his reaction. "I'm not sure of his schedule."

"I've found schedule issues are easily remedied with the right motivation." Fox wanders behind the chief's desk.

"Look, Skip..." Watters tracks the detective, squinting.

Cap smiles sweetly. "We need to go for a drink, Jamie. Go to the Square Grouper. When is the next great cover band playing? They bring in the best cover bands."

"OK," Watters sighs. "Of course. I can call Congressman Harris' Florida office and set an interview up. Skip, I'll attend."

"No problem, Jamie. I would do the same myself. Dr. Argall and I'll wait. Let's make it for today, shall we?"

The police chief shivers and inhales. "Go for coffee, and I'll meet you in our break room."

Fox gets a text from Roofie as they leave the chief's office.

> Call me. No one's hurt. Got info you need.

"I gotta call Roof, Cap."

"No problem. I'll make fresh coffee."

Fox dials Roofie as he paces the small room. "What's up?"

"Ellis, I've got some info from Robby Alvarez. I got it when Tick and I left Detroit to come home. I held it back."

Fox grimaces. "I assume the delay was to manage me."

"It was. As Tick and I were leaving Robby's place, one of his guys came out and handed me a paper with a name. 'Chuck Sams.' The abbreviation for attorney was on it, too."

"Chuck Sams is a friend of Tom Masters."

"Yes, he works in Masters' new firm. Robby told us Tick was — and I quote here—'the mess.' He said 'I don't play with the District.'"

"Your friend Robby is on the right path, but a step or two behind. They would have loved Tick to be 'the mess,' but failed."

"So, DC is involved."

"DC, possibly, and Natalie Forester for certain. And Tom Masters, at least peripherally. Old home week."

"Natalie?"

"Yup. She maneuvered to meet me on the turnpike, and, in her *goumada* nightclub singer kinda way, explained the meth angle was an excuse to harass me. She was unclear about the identity of the harasser."

"I'd strongly consider Natalie herself," Roofie offers.

"Your Detroit information may confirm it. Natalie knows Chuck, and Tom, of course."

"How is she involved in everything else?" Roofie asks. "What does Cap know about Natalie?"

Fox ignores the Cap question. "Well, I suspect she's leading Ann Carley by the string. I'm uncertain. Natalie would never hurt Grace; at least not until she's ready to go nuclear on me. Such a move would declare a war she doesn't want. In fact, I believe Ann may be in some trouble for her action against Grace. Which is an action against me."

Roofie is silent for a few beats. "How's this all connected?"

"News at eleven." Fox wanders out of the break room into the hall, closing the door behind him.

"Tell Cap about Natalie, Ellis. About Tom Masters."

"Cap will overreact. He's never liked Natalie. And he's a control freak. Have you seen his orchid collection?"

twenty-nine
update: orchids do smell

"TODAY at 5:00 p.m. will be perfect, Jamie. Thanks." Cap pats his colleague on the shoulder. "We'll meet you at the congressman's home."

As they leave the Inlet Colony Police Station, Fox points to a police officer walking down another hallway. "Guy!" The detective calls.

The cop turns and hesitates. After too long, he says, "Hello. Lieutenant Argall, right?" He tries to smile but scowls instead.

"Fancy meeting you here. Captain Harley, this is the Jupiter police officer who first examined the Lighthouse scene."

Cap keeps walking. "Well, Officer, you're now our new best friend. Call your superior and say you're coming with Captain Skip Harley of the Palm Beach Sheriff's department. You won't be back at your post today. Have them call me with questions."

"What a fortunate event, running into you. Brilliant." Fox grins as he walks the cop to the door. "Need to use my phone?"

The Sweater Case

Missy meets Cap, Fox, and the Jupiter Police officer at the main door in the lobby. "I need to talk with you for a minute, Captain Harley."

"Let's go to the conference room, Missy." Cap turns to Fox and the Jupiter cop. "You two stay right here. Don't move until I'm back."

Missy and Cap walk to the guest conference room.

"Tick's still in your office. I put the Martin County Deputy in Interview C. This lawyer showed up before the deputy made her call. We're sure she didn't call anyone because we have her phone." The executive assistant frowns. "I wouldn't let the lawyer in. Was I right?"

"We'll discuss details later, Miss, but yes, exactly right. Is the lawyer a woman?"

"Yes, a woman. She's not happy. She... sorta made threats to me."

"Well, she's made a mistake. She's in my house now." He stomps from the conference room.

Approaching Fox and the Jupiter cop, Cap snarls at his lieutenant, "You've lost control of Natalie Forester."

"Forester?" The detective flinches.

Guy the cop startles and runs.

"Catch him!" Cap yells.

Fox and three uniforms take off. It doesn't take long to stop the pudgy, middle-aged man.

As they walk the cop back, Cap says, "I'm not going to cuff you, Officer, but one more move and I'll change my mind. We're dealing with a murder here. Not some fucking personal drama."

The group heads to the elevator for the fourth floor.

"Fox, you go to Interview C, IT room. Go in through the

back hall immediately, with no detours. Officer... What's your name?"

"Morgan. Guy Morgan."

"Officer Morgan, I'm gonna lock you in Interview B, thanks to your sprint. I'll call your super and wait for someone to arrive before interviewing you. My deputies will escort you and confiscate your phone and other items." Cap gestures to the deputies. "Lock him in."

Fox stands still with his head down, staring at his phone. The phone is dark. "Natalie."

"Go to the IT room. No detouring. You never fucking fail to underestimate me, Lieutenant. Never. Fucking. Fail." Cap stalks off.

Missy joins the captain and they walk to the front hall, stopping at Interview C. No one is waiting by the door.

"I told her to wait here." Missy checks the door and peeks in. "She's not in with Deputy Carley."

A dark-haired woman walks out of the restroom into the hall.

"Ma'am? This is my captain." Missy walks toward the woman.

It's not Natalie.

"I need to meet with my client, *tout de suite*, Captain. No more delays."

"We haven't questioned your client, Counselor." Cap shrugs his shoulders to relax. "I have a call into her sheriff."

"I'm here now."

"Nope," Cap decides, striding away. "You may sit in this hallway. Missy will bring you coffee or water. That's the only choice I'm offering. You wait, or you don't. Sue me."

Leslie Youssef stands outside his office, talking with another deputy. "Hey, Captain Harley, Tick... Sergeant Tickman, he's waiting for you."

She throws open the door, and Cap storms in, bumping

into Tick. His injured hand slams into the sergeant's abdomen.

"Fuck! Damn, shit!" Cap jerks away, shaking his bandaged hand. "Dammit, Tick, your freaking stomach is like a fucking rock."

"Hey, I'm sorry. I heard Leslie, and..."

"Go sit down. We've got a lot of details to cover." Cap heads to his orchids.

"I never touched your orchids, but, man, the odor gets to you after a while. How do you stand it?"

"Had a virus a while back. It took out my sense of smell. To jerk your partner around, I told him orchids didn't have any fragrance. He wrote me a fully referenced damn paper, with links you could click." Cap shakes his head. "Fox has this weird brain-olfactory thing. Comes with Asperger's. Shouldn't tease him. I really rounded on him now, and it turns out I was wrong."

"My partner needs yanked back once in a while. I guess I'm still not allowed to play with my friends?"

"We're close to getting you cleared, but not yet. This is about protecting you. No one believes you're involved, but we must be able to prove it." Cap leans back in his chair. "Your partner is about to go through even more stress. I might have screwed up this time, but I can smell Natalie Forester. She's involved in whatever is going on. She's a loon and obsessed with Fox. I'm not sure where this is going."

"This Forester woman attacked Grace?"

"I sincerely doubt it, but I'm not sure. Forester is more about the game of harassing Fox. Hurting Grace? Nah. Physically attacking either of the Argalls would risk and possibly end her recreation. I agree she's behind hurting you."

"Me? Why?"

"Jealousy. You're important to Fox. It's too simple."

"She gone after you?"

"We had our run-ins. Fox and I have a very different relationship. Much more like a—I can't believe I'm saying this—a big brother situation. I protect him and Natalie always wants him protected. From everyone except her." Cap waves his hand at Tick. "You can go home if you'd like. Or you can stay here and do the paperwork I need. Your choice. But you can't go near your partner or any of the interview rooms. Suspects or witnesses are in, and you don't want any run-ins in case you end up deposed or interviewed by anyone beyond me. Right?"

Tick makes a growling noise but nods his head. "Give me my assignments."

thirty
cartoon cinderella and the pretend prince

A VIOLIN PLAYS, AND 'HELD' flows out of the sanctuary. Jacob Moreno leaves his desk to knock on Roofie's door.

"Come, Jacob." Roofie's voice cracks. "Come in."

Tears streak the pastor's faded and drawn face.

"Roof. She's been playing for hours. Should we...?"

"No. No, we'll let Marley grieve her way. She'll stop when she's ready. You and I pray for her revelation. I'm wondering about the violin, though. I'd expect her to play piano."

"Piano?" Jacob sits down, inviting his old friend to share. "Talk out loud, Roof."

"The violin was Marley's first instrument. I remember the day. Her seventh birthday—" Roofie's eyes darken in the memory. "She got her first adult-sized violin. She's always been tall."

He breaks down and puts his head in his arms on the desk.

Jacob leans over to his friend, praying out loud. "Lord, we serve You, and You alone are sacred in our lives. We receive revelation and our healing."

"I'll wait until she plays the piano." His words slur in pain. "Then, I'll join her."

Late in the afternoon, the piano begins. Marley's playing 'Held' again. The song is a theme for her grief.

Time to talk.

Roofie joins the song as he walks into the sanctuary.

Marley falters. She stops playing and starts again, trying to sing. Her voice washes out in her tears.

The struggle on her beautiful face. Her father's face.

After a moment, her long-learned resolve rises and steel replaces the anguish as she continues the song. He drags a bench behind her and sings softly, joining her to the finale.

"You're my beloved child, my only child." He wraps his arms around her. She collapses against his chest. "I may not share your physical DNA, but you're mine. It's time to talk. About a lot of things. Past the time to talk out loud."

"I don't think I can."

"OK, I will. We'll start with your parents."

Marley turns to her godfather. "My parents?"

"Oh, yes, Marls, your parents. We're starting at the beginning. We're going to talk."

"Out loud." She repeats the favorite phrase of her Uncle Roofie.

"Out loud. You aren't my sweet child anymore. You're an adult, a mother. A wife." He holds her tighter as he reminds her of her loss.

Unfathomable loss.

She stiffens in his arms; the familiar willpower surging in to hide every disappointment.

"You were told so many times, Marls. 'You're your father's daughter.' And you are, in so many ways. Your father's good ways. You monitored and collected them. Spun them into your own resolute character."

Marley chokes, tears flowing.

The Sweater Case

"But you're also your mother, her goodness, her caring. You learned how to give from your mother. You offer the core of who you are to everyone. Your giving nature is your center, not the many gifts your father gave you. Those are fences and flowers, sweetheart. Do you understand what I mean?"

Shaking her head, she leans against him. "Sounds like an 'Uncle Roof Fancy.'"

Roofie laughs. "Well, I recognize the description. Yes, one of my 'fancies,' for certain. Most of us spend a lifetime building a theme for ourselves, for better or worse. I call it a 'banner,' the Life Statement. Our banner colors every decision we make. It drives us down certain roads."

"And my banner is 'Giving?'"

"Something close." Roofie runs his hand down her black, curly hair. "You figure out the details. It's between you and your God, in the end. The gifts we're given? We have both fences—your spiritual, moral, and mental structures—and flowers, your musical talent, your brain, to offer beauty and fragrance for our hard walk."

"Fences and flowers. A perfect Uncle Roofie analogy."

"Work on finding the word on your banner, Marls. God gave us words for a reason. The specific words matter, like in a lyric or a poem. One is perfect, and another, so close, misses the mark."

"So, what's my dad's banner?'"

"Ah, you'd think I'd know, of all people?" Roofie pats her cheek. "I might come close, I suppose, but just a guess. At best, I can make an observation. My opinion is 'Duty.' Your dad's a wonderful man. I love him as I love few others. You chose Josh because he reflected your dad in so many ways."

She lays her head on the piano and sobs.

"But your dad's passion is to duty, Marls, because duty is a rule, and rules can be memorized and followed by rote. Rules are your dad's forté. He understands them and uses them to negotiate what is to him a senseless social world."

"Duty drives him?"

"I suspect it does. 'Responsibility' is different from duty. It actively changes, moment to moment, evolving with the situation. Responsibility demands an active awareness of others your dad simply doesn't have."

"He can't reach that, can he?"

"I don't think he can. We have a name for your dad's lack of social awareness. We assigned it a label. The truth is, we all need a label."

"To go with our banner?" Marley's smile is sadness itself.

"Yes, yes," he chuckles, squeezing his goddaughter. "A banner proclaims, and a label warns. If you think about it, they're both warnings. Humans are two-sided coins."

"'We sin most in the areas of our gifts.'"

"You listen to my sermons?" Roofie pokes Marley in her ribs. "Yes, and your parents are caricatures in the statement's proof. God taught me immeasurably by knowing your parents. As they raised you, they were raising themselves. They were so young, Marls. Maybe too young, but we got you, our precious girl."

Marley sighs. "I spent the last few years—years with Josh —tearing my life apart, examining my conflicted observations and feelings about my parents."

"What did you discover?"

"I was always on the outside, my nose pressed against the frosted window, looking in at the sparkling, glorious Prince's Ball. Following my mother as she danced. Studying my red-haired Cinderella, who charms them all and wins the Prince."

"Except the Prince won, Marls. And he knows it."

"Josh helped me manage everything. He loved my parents. He understood and valued them."

"And he'll always be your help, even as you continue on

your alternative path. Let's worship, sweet girl. We'll give praise for your Josh and honor him. You play, and we'll sing. Remember what I said. Your dad's aware he won. He has been for many years. Understand him as another human. Not some cartoon hero. Not a Prince."

thirty-one
gimbal stable, what?

CAP ENTERS the tech room of Interview C to find Fox leaning against the back wall playing Brick Breaker.

"Has he ignored you, Ty?"

Tyler laughs. "Nah, he talks and plays his game all at the same time."

"What have you been talking about?" Cap sits beside the IT specialist.

"Gimbal stabilizers."

Cap rolls his eyes. "Right. Well, let's talk about Deputy Carley, instead. Fox, you feed me questions, but you will not own this interview. I'll ask what I want, *capisce*?"

Fox doesn't answer.

"Glad we understand each other. Tyler, Dr. Argall is not to leave this room. I've put two deputies outside the door. If Fox gets... destabilized, you hit the emergency buzzer. Yes?"

"Hilarious," Fox mumbles.

"Glad you liked. This interview is only one piece of a bigger puzzle. We remember our chess match."

"You're on a roll this afternoon."

"Right? I feel pretty cheeky." Cap drags himself up from the chair and opens the door. "Listen, this is going to be a long-ass day with lots of opportunities to lose our shit if we are so inclined. I'm not inclined. Keep your shit together so I can."

Cap enters the Interview Room and puts his hands on the table. "Hello, Deputy Carley. For the taped record, I'm Captain Skip Harley. We have met. You're detained on suspicion of kidnapping. We contacted your supervisor, Howell Farling. He's aware we're interviewing you."

Carley sits stiffly in the metal chair. Her nose is purple and clearly broken or out of joint.

"We offered medical treatment for your injury and you declined, correct? Please answer out loud for the record."

"Yes."

"How did you injure your nose? Please explain your injury."

"No, thanks."

"You're aware we found Grace Argall's phone in your personal trash can? Inside your home?"

"No."

"Well, we did. Can you explain how Dr. Grace Argall's phone got in your trash?"

"No."

"Luckily, I can. Twenty-first century easy, actually. Your teen-aged neighbor videotaped you and an unidentified colleague 'walking' Grace Argall 'Weekend at Bernie's' style through the alley. Grace appears unconscious."

Ann turns away, swallowing hard.

Stan Baskins walks in. "I'm..."

"I know who you are," Ann says, voice flat.

"Your turn to explain this debacle. Arrive before the crowd." Stan sits beside Ann.

"She was drunk. Dumb bitch broke my nose."

"Good for her. But, here's the thing, Ann," Stan says. "We found Grace. Zero alcohol in her system. Drugged, yes, but injected with heroin. You're in a terrible place. Your companion is in the other room. A chatty, nervous dude. I just finished interviewing him."

"I want to talk with Howell." Carley's eyes dart between the men.

Cap sits in the chair across from the deputy. "The sheriff has seen the video, and you're suspended with the intention to terminate. The video is crystal clear, Ann. What the hell were you thinking?"

"Guy Morgan." Stan taps his fingers on the table. "He folded before I asked him the first question. He's terrified of the people he believes are running the entire meth operation."

"Stupid bastard."

Stan shrugs. "Another interview coming in the next hours will add a lot of information to our picture. Last chance, Deputy. Captain Harley doesn't like dirty cops any more than I do, and we always argue about who we're voting for in the 'confess and earn a deal' sweepstakes."

"You aren't even on my list of worries," Ann mutters.

Fox's voice pops into Cap's earpiece. "Ask her about Natalie. Ask her, 'Are you OK with Natalie leaving you exposed as a sacrifice?'"

"Natalie left you exposed. A sacrifice. How is that OK?"

Ann's eyes dilate and she shakes, unable to keep her hands still.

Continuing, Cap asks, "You had to believe Fox Argall would look everywhere and at everyone for his wife. You bought a house practically next door. How smart is attacking Grace?"

"I didn't plan to attack Grace." Ann puts her face down on her arms. "I didn't want the damn house. Buying the place was trouble."

Fox says into Cap's earpiece, "How do you think Natalie

will react when she finds out you gave Grace Argall a fatal dose of heroin?"

Cap repeats the question to Ann. "How will Natalie react when she finds out you gave Grace Argall a fatal dose of heroin?"

The deputy's shoulders shudder as she breaks down. She has dark stains under her arms, and the sour odor of sweat fills the room. Without lifting her head, she says, "Grace showed up on my porch. I have no idea why she was there. Morgan and I opened the door and walked out before we noticed her. The girl we had, the mule's twin. We tied her in the living room, out in the open on the floor. Grace spotted her. We didn't want to hurt anyone. The damned woman took off, and I just wanted to talk to her. She jumped me in her bathroom."

Fox mutters, "My girl."

"Where is Dalia?" Cap leans into Ann's face. "Don't add another murder on your charges. Tell me she's still alive."

"She was alive. We never hurt her. She—she went crazy. We had to tie her."

"Where is she? Where is Dalia?"

"Guy took her to the Inlet Colony." Ann shakes in spasms. "I don't know anything. I'm not a part of anything with the meth! Guy shot the Argall woman up. He did that shit on his own, dragged me into it."

Fox whispers in Cap's earpiece. "Who is Natalie to you?"

"How are you connected to Natalie Forester? Who's Natalie to you?"

Ann closes her eyes and presses her lips together. "Natalie's my sister."

thirty-two
the gang's all here and they're not happy

THE GATES to the sprawling mansion crawl open, allowing the police cruiser to enter a stunning property with endless views of the Atlantic Ocean. As they head toward the bright yellow house, two motorcycles come and ride beside them.

"Well, this is a first." Cap snorts. "A fifty-foot escort."

"It's a fifty-foot threat," Fox murmurs.

"If only they knew how you took to threats."

"Like you're somehow mild-mannered. Well, they're about to find out. I won't leave here without a U.S. Congressman unless we find a lot of answered questions."

"Do you think a federal agent is the best provocation at this point?" Stan watches the motorcycles swerve to the sides of the car. "Should I wait out here? Those guys probably carried my credentials at some point."

"No offense, Stan, but these guys are more likely straight from in-country to mercenary."

"I meant my Force Recon creds."

"Ah, well, crikey. And they say I'm over-qualified. But none of it matters." Fox finishes his current game and drops his device in his pocket. "We leave here knowing this is a federal case, not a simple local murder. Mark me."

The men leave the cruiser and walk to the front door. The two motorcycles remain next to the police car.

As they approach the bright red door, it opens, and Jamie Watters walks onto the veranda.

"Jamie, glad you're all prepared." Cap narrows his eyes at the Inlet Colony Chief. "Meet Stan Baskins, FBI out of Miami."

"Yes, I believe I met Stan. Congressman Harris can give you about half an hour." Watters coughs, his cheeks turning pink.

Cap laughs. "Fair warning. The congressman will give us the time we need, Jamie. He has no rank in this investigation, and no consideration beyond the courtesy already received."

Alexi Gardarov stands like a statue in the octagonal foyer, wearing a dark tee shirt stretched on his muscular frame under a tight black jacket and a side arm bulge. An earpiece snakes down the back of his neck.

"If I understood when I was twelve that valets—butlers—could dress like James Bond, I might never have made it to medical school." Fox walks up and leans into Alexi's personal space. "Where are your sunglasses? You need sunglasses."

"Fox, behave yourself." Cap smiles at the security man. "Mr. Gardarov? Forgive my detective. To be honest, he's a little disgruntled. Irritated. He discovered you lied to him on his last visit. Dr. Argall hates to be lied to. Hates it."

"'Detests' is a better word, Cap. Words mean things, y'know?" The detective has his phone back out and the Brick Breaker tune chirps in the background. "A deeply personal affront to me."

Gardarov doesn't reply. He turns and leads them into a study on the right at the far end of the foyer. He pushes the door further open, showing a tanned, white-haired man seated behind a massive mahogany desk.

"Good grief, Leona. We've walked into the detective noir

you were barking about, Cap." Fox strides to the desk and slumps into a dark red leather chair in front of it, never looking up from his game.

"Who is Leona, Fox?" Stan asks.

"Leona was his grandmother." Cap takes the seat beside his lieutenant, leaving the FBI agent to stand behind them.

Stan moves to the right side of the room, with a view of the open door.

Fox smiles vacantly, immersed in his game. "She was a Northern Diva. Charming as the sun sparkling on the dew, with no filter whatsoever."

"Explains some things." Cap leans over and offers his hand to the congressman. "Forgive our personal conversation, sir. We're grateful for the opportunity to speak with you about our local murder."

"Anytime, of course, Captain Harley." Michael Harris shakes Cap's hand but regards Fox with an empty smile. "From the accent, I assume this is our famous Dr. Argall?"

"Yup. And this is—" Cap points to Stan, but Fox interrupts.

"You made me unhappy, Mr. Harris. Upset."

The congressman flushes pink, his jaw flexing.

Cap ignores his subordinate. "And this is Stan Baskins, FBI out of Miami. Gentlemen, meet our U.S. Congressman, Michael Harris."

Harris is still staring at Fox. He stands and strolls in front of the detective and sits on the edge of his desk. Leaning forward, he says quietly, "I was so sorry to learn of your son-in-law's death, Dr. Argall. Oh, and your wife's accident, of course. Bad days for you. So sorry."

Fox shifts but continues to play Brick Breaker. The room is thick for too long, and Stan moves a step forward. The detective glances up at the FBI agent, and relaxes back in his chair, stretching his long legs out to the congressman's desk.

Harris slides away from Fox's shoes, which brush his trousers.

"Dr. Argall appreciates such personal attention from our elected officials," Cap says.

"Yes," Fox agrees. "With such a detailed understanding of all the minor events surrounding our murder investigation, I'm certain you will be cracking excellent help to us in other, far more important areas."

The congressman turns his back to the men, facing the wall of glass doors to the ocean. "Captain Harley, any questions for me?"

"Yes, thank you, we do. Dr. Argall has the more acute connection to the case, of course, as the senior investigating officer."

"And the original officer at the scene," Fox offers.

"Lieutenant, you weren't the first one to the scene. Remember Officer Guy?" Cap says. "Guy Morgan?"

"*Mae hwnna'a gywir!*" [Is that correct!] Fox stands and stretches, laying his phone on the congressman's desk. "*Sut gallwn i anghofio?* [How could I forget?] Guy. Guy Morgan. The Jupiter Police Officer."

Cap stands and leans on the back of his chair. "*Yn union.* [Exactly.] Guy Morgan. Congressman Harris, have you met Guy?"

"I don't generally meet patrol officers." Harris grinds his teeth. "Guy Morgan? No, I'm certain I've not heard the name."

"See, odd, right?" Fox wanders to the glass wall and stops beside Harris. "Guy is currently our guest over at Violent Crimes. Stan, you should explain this part."

"More my thing, for sure. Guy Morgan is in federal custody on suspicion of trafficking methamphetamine and obstruction of justice. He's adamant you all have intimate relationships. He's close with you." Stan gestures to the bodyguard. "You and your buddy over here, Alexi."

"Yup," Cap agrees. "Congressman Harris, the thing is, we're gonna need a full interview, and I'm afraid everything will have to be taped. To protect us all."

"Are you accusing me of something?"

"Bloody cliché," Fox mutters, shooting his cuffs. "Back in the noir."

Gardarov steps inside the door.

"The gang's all here." The detective swipes his phone off the desk and walks out past the man. "I'll be in the car."

"We'll need your time as well, Mr. Gardarov," Cap adds. "Let's accompany the congressman for an interview right now. We'll go to my department, if that's OK, Agent Baskins? It's closer for the congressman than a trip to Miami."

"Sure, Captain Harley."

Cap gestures to the police chief, who was silent throughout the exchange. "Jamie, I forgot you were here. You're free to join us. In fact, I insist."

thirty-three
crikey, that was unexpected

SKIP HARLEY STANDS in the IT room of Interview C, fixing his earpiece. "Ticker, you may listen to the interview. If anything pops into your head, run your thought by Stan. Stan, you and I agree you'll stay in here until one of us finds the best opportunity for you to enter the interview?"

"Yes," Stan agrees. "I'll come in by your flag. When appropriate, I'll assist with arrests. OK? You good with allowing Harris and Watters in the same interview?"

"Yup." Cap taps Tyler's shoulder. "Ty, I expect a group in this room. Representative Harris' crew will be larger than we're used to hosting. We need to use home-field advantage in our tight space. Any problems you see for your end?"

"No, just try not to talk over each other." Tyler grins. "Spread people out, if you can."

"Right. It's my room, and I'm in control. Fox, do we agree on the choreography? Any last thoughts?"

"I doubt the lawyers will be fully informed of their clients' dubious activities. We should be able to use their ignorance in our favor."

"Tyler, I expect good behavior from Dr. Argall, but stay

awake. Ticker will recognize any tantrums coming and warn you."

Fox rolls his eyes. "Tyler recognizes the volatile one here."

The technician puts his head down and laughs. "My job is like watching a TV mystery show."

"OK, people. We're on." Cap leads the lieutenant into the interview room, where Michael Harris sits at the table, lawyers on both sides. Jamie Watters sits in the corner, squirming.

"Welcome to my house, Congressman," Cap announces. "Let me know if you need anything to make you comfortable."

Fox strolls to a chair and sits across from Michael Harris, stretching his legs in front of him.

Cap motions to Fox. "Note my detective's not on his phone game. Bodes an interesting time. No one actually wants Dr. Argall to pay all his attention to them."

One of Harris' lawyers, an auburn-haired woman in her thirties, scoffs. "Intimidation By Subordinate, Captain? Really." She stares down at her stack of papers, which are separated by dozens of sherbet-colored sticky notes.

The door opens, and a man with bright red hair enters the interview room. "Don't underestimate Ellis Argall, *cherie*."

Fox grins, lop-sided, and stands to hold his hand out. "Well. Look at you, mate. Haven't seen you in forever."

The man shakes the detective's hand and nods to the room. "I'm going to need some introductions. Is this your boss, El? I need to meet him for drinks sometime and bitch about you. First things first. Why have you invited my client to your lovely but oh-so-official interview room?"

"As lovely as this gathering is, I intend to manage the interview my way." Cap rolls his finger in the air, signaling Tyler.

The man chuckles. "Of course, of course. Just happy to visit my old colleague. Your house, Captain Harley."

"Fox, give your friend your chair." Cap motions to the

mirror. "Ready the tape. We don't want to keep anyone longer than necessary."

"Before I steal your chair, Dr. Argall, I'd like a moment with my colleagues. No need to leave the room. We'll cluster in this corner." His smile is dazzling.

"Take your time, Chuck," Fox says. "Oh, Cap, forgive me. This is Chuck Sams, Esquire."

"Chuck Sams," Tick groans in the IT room. "My partner's shaking this lawyer's hand? Fuck."

Tyler barely reacts. "Sergeant Tickman, Cap only told me to worry about Lieutenant Argall, not you."

"Do you have a problem, Tick?" Stan frowns. "What about Chuck Sams?"

"The red-haired guy. Fuck."

"You better spit it out," Stan says.

"I took my vacation in Detroit." The sergeant balls up his fists. "Reverend Parks and me."

"OK, that's weird. I didn't realize you were close with Roofie. Do I need to stop the interview?"

"Fox sent us to some of Roofie's old friends. We weren't welcome."

"Fox sent you where? You're going to have to help me. Roofie's old friends?" Stan backs up to the door. "What do we need to do here?"

Tick leans against the wall and closes his eyes. "The Argalls and the Parks, they met in Columbus, Ohio. Roofie was a drug dealer. Among other things."

"A drug dealer," Ty mutters. "Rev. Parks was a drug dealer?"

"Roof and I went to talk to one of his old companions. Anyway, the guy wasn't happy with Roofie showing up. He said I was trouble, and DC was involved. He kicked us out. As we left, two of his thugs followed us. One gave us a piece of paper with a scrawled name."

"Lemme guess." Stan groans.

"Chuck Sams," Tyler says, staring at Tick.

"Who is this guy, other than someone from everyone's past? What's your partner's relationship with Sams?"

"He's a lawyer at Fox's old firm in Boston."

"So?" Stan relaxes. "We just tell Cap and Fox. He's a lawyer. Boston, that's a bit off, but probably has a DC office. Clearly involved, as he's here. You didn't tell anyone about the note?"

"Slipped my mind. It's been a crazy two and a half days. Tom Masters headed up Fox's law firm and represented Senator Conway, the murderer."

"Conway?"

"Conway. He stalked Fox and attacked children to get his attention."

"I am so missing a story here," Stan says. "Well, large firms represent important people. Might mean nothing. Tyler, give me comm to the earpieces. We're fine, everyone breathe."

"You got it, Agent. Give it ten seconds and you're live."

Stan waits for the thumbs up and speaks into Fox and Cap's earpieces. "Hey, guys. On the trip Tick took to Detroit, Chuck Sams' name came up. Do we need to adjust? Or?"

Cap glares at the mirror.

"Chuck!" Fox chirps. "You're representing Fuzzy Whalin? He's hilarious, don't you think?"

The group turns and stares at the detective. Michael Harris wheezes and chokes, and throws up all over his lawyers.

"Crikey. Seems like an overreaction."

thirty-four
fuzzy whalin is not your ordinary farmer

"WHERE ARE OUR ERST-WHILE CRIMINALS, MISSY?" Cap sits in his office with the team. "We lose anyone?"

Missy reads off her list. "Interview Room C is being cleaned, and you ordered Congressman Harris moved to Interview A. He is alone; he hasn't requested an attorney. We sent a physician to check him over. Ann Carley, the deputy, is now in isolated lock-up. Guy Morgan is in Interview D, the small room. Alexi Gardarov is still in Interview B."

They all turn to Fox, who sits in a corner playing with his phone and ignores them.

"Thanks, Miss." Cap throws a wadded piece of paper at his detective and hits the table in front of him. Fox puts his phone in his lap. "Lieutenant, we need to discuss this comment of yours about Fuzzy Whalin. Seems to be nauseatingly on the mark. What brought it on?"

"I'm pondering the threads. Even I need some alone time to think. You lot demand too much from me." Fox squirms in his seat, rolling his phone between his fingers. "Fuzzy Whalin is a major drug thug from Gwinnett County, Georgia. Tick and Roof were planning to meet him on the way back from Detroit, but Fuzzy was unavailable."

"Not in anyone's report." Cap glares at Tick.

The sergeant stares at his shoes, frowning.

Fox flicks his green eyes at the ceiling. "No need to start blaming. All null data from the Georgia leg of the trip. We learned nothing from Whalin being unavailable. Roofie was dropping in, without notice, so his lack of availability doesn't tell us anything. He may've been busy. Otherwise engaged. We have to ignore it and not assign any value."

"The unofficial team on this unofficial trip was your partner and subordinate and—at the time, the only fucking suspect in our crime, accompanied by your best friend and crony." Cap's face flashes red. *"Nid yw hyn drosodd,* Fox." [This isn't over, Fox.]

The detective snickers. "Roof as my crony. He might not like the description."

"Dammit, Fox!" Cap slams his fist on the table. "I'm not done dealing with all your manipulations in this case. I *am* going to return to the subject. Now, fucking pay attention. Why did you expect a reaction from the Harris group to the Whalin question?"

"I happened to be talking to an old friend from my Boston law firm. A crack legal assistant; she was always helpful. You may remember her from the Conway representation. Anyway, she mentioned Chuck had a 'new client.' Said he was '400 pounds if he was an ounce.' She wondered aloud if he could afford the legal fees as he was dressed in 'farmer overalls,' and they 'weren't even new.'"

"And this description screamed Fuzzy Whalin to you?"

The detective finishes his game and faces the group. "Yes. Fuzzy is a different sort than most of his competitors. He's not a business person, just a psychopath who enjoys killing people. Years ago, he discovered inducing fear opened doors. Doors to

The Sweater Case

easy money. Spends a lot of time farming his own land. Only God knows what's buried on the acreage. My law clerk friend mentioned 'the farmer' met with Chuck and some senior partners. I took a runner."

"Took a runner," Cap growls.

Fox chuckles. "Didn't expect the reaction we got. I was harassing Chuck, trying to put him off his game. Whatever his game is."

"So, where do we go now? What's the best next step?" Stan asks.

"Next step is talking with Michael Harris alone, if he'll agree." Fox shrugs, going back to his game. "We have to separate him from Chuck, at least. You'd think we're a move ahead, but I'm never sure."

"You and Stan go in with Harris." Cap walks to the door and turns. "I'll be in the IT room. Don't go off script, Dr. Argall. Leave the room and discuss anything with your colleagues and me if you want to change course. This is a U.S. congressman. How do we manage him?"

Fox puts his phone in his pocket. "Harris isn't an attorney. He's a teacher with a trust fund; one who has never set foot in a classroom. He's used to an easier life than he's wandered into. I guarantee he's terrified."

"So you intend to scare him more?" Cap sighs.

"Well, maybe Stan will want to scare him. I'll consider it a victory if he throws up again. May be my new standard for interviewing bad guys." The detective straightens his tie and buttons his coat. "I love this part."

Stan and Fox enter the interview room as the duty physician is finishing up with Harris.

"BP coming down, Dr. Kirk?" Fox asks.

"Yes, returning to normal, Dr. Argall. Denies chest pain, no fever, no rash. Blood pressure is higher—170 over 85, but within the normal range for someone agitated. Heart rate 80. My diagnosis is acute anxiety."

"I'm fine." Harris grits his teeth.

The physician hesitates and asks, "Are you comfortable with me leaving you, sir? Dr. Argall's a licensed physician."

Harris waves his hand, his face flushing. "Yes, go on. I'll need my attorneys before we restart any interview."

"I wondered if the room got a bit too warm for you." Stan sits down, concern etching his face. "Too many in the room at once? Let's limit the number of people this time. Which attorney would you like, Congressman Harris?"

"Yes, I agree, Stan." Fox frowns, circling the table. "The room was stifling. Mr. Harris might want to choose amongst his team. I assume you want Chuck for sure, as he traveled all this way to be here for you?"

The detective sits in the chair beside Harris, leaning in on the man. "Unless my friend Chuck ran down here from Gwinnett? Much shorter trip. He spends a lot of time in northern Georgia these days."

The congressman groans and puts his head down.

"Mr. Harris, did you request Chuck Sams? Or did he show up here unannounced?"

"Is he representing your interests or someone else's?" Stan taps the table. "Think."

"Stan and I are worried about you," Fox says. "Alexi is being asked about the meth distribution right now. Add murder. Officer Guy's yapping away as we sit here."

"Don't forget the connection to Fuzzy Whalin," Stan adds. "The major drug connection in the southern quarter of the country."

"Yes," Fox murmurs. "To be truthful, well, not entirely in your best interest, this."

Harris sits up and breathes in, trying to recover. "No, you're correct. Sams is unnecessary, Dr. Argall."

The Sweater Case

"Did you send for him? Is he here on your request? I must say, I'm missing the 'in your best interest' part."

Closing his eyes, Harris mumbles, "I need to speak to the District Attorney."

Stan exhales and sits back. "The DA is not holding any federal cards, Representative Harris. I am."

Fox gets up and strolls behind Harris. "The murder charge is local, of course, but the meth distribution is definitely federal. Stan, here, he's the man to sort cartel jazz. Would you like to focus on the drugs?"

The congressman moans.

"Again, being brutal, Chuck Sams is a drug lawyer. He's likely to be less than interested in a dead girl on your charge sheet."

"No, no. No." Harris chokes and coughs. "I have no part in any murder."

"No murder, only the meth?" Stan asks. "We're pretty sure on the meth thing. The murder, you don't think the congressman is involved, do you, Lieutenant?"

"Dr. Argall," Harris says, "I would never be involved in any harm to another human."

"Yeah, meth never hurt anyone." Fox waits a moment. "Congressman Harris, you're on the Homeland Security Committee, right? Who told you about my wife?"

Harris' mouth opens, and his pupils dilate.

Stan flips his palms up on the table. "Deputy Carley? Guy? Or was it Natalie who told you?"

"Natalie...?" Harris stammers. "I don't know a Natalie."

Fox leans back on the table close to the man. "Wouldn't have been Natalie who told you, Congressman Harris, because Natalie wouldn't have countenanced harming my wife, much less giving her a fatal overdose of heroin."

Harris gags and chokes, dry-heaving off the side of his chair. "Fatal... No one said..."

"Yes, fatal dose, Michael," Fox whispers. "I'll never stop haunting the lives of anyone involved."

Tears roll down Harris' cheeks.

"No one has a deal yet, Mr. Harris. Do yourself a favor." Stan pushes himself up from the chair. "The entire game is over. Falling apart at the seams. Start by answering one question at a time. Easy. Start by telling us about the dead girl."

Harris bursts into sobs. "Deanna. I loved her. I wanted to save her. Dalia wanted to save her."

thirty-five
truth is complicated

FOX STANDS with Cap in the IT room off Interview D as Stan interrogates Guy. "We agree Tick's not involved, but we need a confession to eliminate the DNA evidence. We need Dalia."

Guy the cop chatters away to Stan about finding the sweater on the Inlet Light, spinning a vague mishmash.

"You're in fear for your life, Guy," Stan urges. "And that's the smartest thing you're thinking so far. You're in a mess. Clear this up for yourself."

The Jupiter police officer's voice cracks and he moans. "My problem with you is minor compared to what they'll do to me."

Fox shuffles in his dance, flipping his phone from hand to hand. "He's frightened of the drug cartel. We must distract him."

"Too bad we can't use Ticker," Cap scowls. "He'd be more effective with a beat cop than a scary FBI agent or an overqualified senior investigator."

"Or an impeccably connected captain of Palm Beach Violent Crimes."

"Maybe you could remember the fact more frequently."

Fox snorts. "These people think Grace is dead. We can use it with Guy. Carley was involved in the assault on Gracie, and we can assume Guy was, too. Florida has the death penalty. He's afraid of the drug cartel, but how easy will prison be for a cop? The goal is to find Dalia. Carley said they tied her when she 'went crazy.' Let me go in, the bereaved husband."

"And that won't scare him?" Cap shakes his head. "Carley and Morgan seem to be worker bees to me. We want the big picture."

"He's already terrified. My issue with him is personal. It changes the type of fear. I know what we need from him. I'll bear everything in mind."

Cap waves his lieutenant out the door. "I'm not sure I agree, but have at it. We gotta break him."

Stan and Morgan glance up as Fox steps in and hovers by the door.

"Dr. Argall, Guy admits he put the sweater on the Inlet Light. He has a memory lapse beyond leaving the material."

"My Gracie was injected with a fatal dose of heroin. I'm a bit past the sweater," Fox murmurs. He doesn't move, eyes on the cop. "I expected the suspect cuffed to the table."

"Cuffed?" Stan's mouth wrinkles in concern. "Uh, wait, man. Might be better if the captain came in, Lieutenant."

"We're fine."

"Where's Cap?" Stan turns to the mirror.

Guy Morgan twists in his seat, motioning to the mirror. "Where's the captain?"

"Why isn't the prisoner cuffed to the table?" Fox leans back and taps his head against the wall. His eyes are bloodshot and ringed with shadows. A two-day scruff covers his sharp jaw, and his curly, dark hair flies up in all directions.

Thump. Thump.

"Come over into the video feed, Lieutenant Argall. Join us at the table so you're on tape. For the record." Stan shifts his weight on the chair. He gestures at the mirror again. "Captain, want to join us?"

"Cap is with Jamie Watters. He took Tyler to tape the chief. The IT room isn't occupied." Fox tilts his head and asks again, "Why is the prisoner not cuffed?"

"I didn't hurt anyone," Guy cries. "I didn't come after you, Lieutenant. Jamie Watters is a tool. Literally and figuratively. You have to understand who's doing this."

"I'll tell you what, Guy." Fox draws out the name, leaning into his Welsh accent. "You came after me and mine. You've got five minutes to explain every single detail. Five minutes. Agent Baskins, you're free to stay or to go. Make your choice now."

"I'm not leaving this prisoner, my prisoner, here alone with you, without a taped interview." Stan pushes to his feet and points. "Lieutenant Argall—"

"Whatever suits," Fox growls. "Officer Morgan, I detest dirty coppers. You came after me and my family. Here's your only deal. You have four minutes and 30 seconds. I have you on three murders. Death penalty cases. No federal cushy for you. You've one chance to take something off the table. The first words I want to hear? Where Dalia is located right this moment."

Morgan flips between the detective and Stan. The FBI agent's face is bright red and getting redder.

"I dumped her on the street. Threw her out. She was out of control."

Fox's expression is set, like an eagle eyeing prey. "Now. Tell me about the drugs. I know about Whalin—the connection to the DC law firm. I want the rest. Who, what, where. Four minutes."

"You've got to help me," the cop keens, rocking in his chair. "It's Harris. It's all his doing. Harris opened a trail for cartel members in Detroit through a corrupt Homeland Security team he runs in Mexico. Protected by a mercenary team of Harris' choosing. I'm not on the inside team. I don't *have* more details. Watters said Fuzzy Whalin was on the warpath because he was cut out of some new deal."

Thump. Fox bangs his head against the door. *Thump.* "I don't like you."

"Agent Baskins," Guy Morgan begs, reaching for Stan's hands.

"You have a lot more for me. Much more." The detective walks along the wall behind Morgan. "You set up the fake scene at the Inlet Light. I want everything. John Tickman. I'm losing my already limited patience. I don't like you. I want to know all about Deanna. Three minutes."

"Wait, Fox. This isn't how—" Stan starts.

"Shut up, Agent Baskins. I've nothing to lose here. The deal with Fuzzy is blown. You saw Chuck Sams, Fuzzy's high-powered personal lawyer, here at the department. Whalin's gonna walk, probably already left the building. Just stay clear of me."

"I can't be present for this."

"There's the door. Your choice, Agent. Leave or stay. Morgan, two minutes and thirty seconds."

Thump.

Morgan grabs Stan's hands. "As an FBI agent, you have to protect me."

"I can't stay here for this." Stan jerks his hands away.

"Two minutes."

"Fuzzy Whalin will butcher us all," Guy Morgan moans.

"You're right. That's a much better idea." Fox throws open the door. "You aren't restrained, Guy. Walk out of here. Get out of my interview room."

"I can't go out there!" Morgan wails. "OK, OK. Carley and I work for Watters. Watters works for Harris. Deanna was Harris' mistress. She worked as a mule for Whalin. Deanna was connected to Whalin from the beginning. Harris? The stupid bastard is clueless. Thought he was a genius because he inherited money and bragged about how he parlayed into a power position inside a cartel while he held an elected federal position."

"Where did Harris meet Deanna?" Stan asks.

"Harris met Deanna at a dance club, for fuck's sake. Fuzzy set the asshole up. Moron had no idea his girlfriend was on Whalin's payroll. Moved her into his damn house! She was playing both sides."

Fox pulls the chair out beside Morgan and pushes it against his leg. "You had Dalia at the yellow house."

"OK, alright. OK. Whalin showed up at Harris' fucking house with Deanna's twin one day. How did her fucking twin hook up with Whalin? I had dumped her on the street. Where was that James Bond wannabe always guarding Harris? Fuzzy just walked in like he had a key."

"Maybe he did," Fox mutters.

Morgan lays his head on the table and continues. "The girls freaked everyone out. Deanna was legit nuts, and her twin was furious at everyone. Fighting."

"Why did Whalin show up? What did he want from Harris?" Stan asks.

"Fuzzy wanted the protection he had in Mexico expanded to Columbia, and wanted the whole deal moved to him. Everyone started arguing. Whalin backhanded Deanna, and all hell broke loose."

Fox pulls the door closed. "What did Deanna's twin do?"

"The twin went for Carley, threw a double-hand blast to her face, and kept going at Fuzzy himself. Whalin shoved her aside and laughed, and then he shot Deanna point blank. The woman was dead before she hit the ground. The twin went wild. Pounded on Deanna's chest, shrieking, trying to restart her heart. Blood flew everywhere. Whalin stood laughing. That's it; nothing else. Except I'm a dead man."

"John Tickman?" Stan asks.

"Who? Who's Tickman?"

"You were a dead man the minute you joined this mess instead of stopping it. The truth is, you were dead way before." Fox flicks his hands to the mirror. "Cap, done here."

Stan smiles at Morgan and follows the detective out.

"You're a good actor, for an FBI flunky." Fox pats the agent on the shoulder.

"Thanks. It helps that I really don't trust you."

thirty-six
who cares what lawyers think?

WHEN FOX ENTERS the glassed office, Cap is leaning forward over the elaborate orchid stand. "Not quite done, Skip."

"No, not quite. We haven't found Dalia. We got most of them. We've got some threads to tie up. I sent officers to Harris' house, his office, and Jamie Watters' home and various places of business."

Silence fills the room. Three days are forever for a missing person. The chances of survival were low even without the description of Deanna's death and the obvious threat from Fuzzy Whalin.

"Let me talk to Watters," Fox argues. "I can get him to tell me his side."

"Watters has representation, and they've requested—demanded—you not be involved in his interrogation. His story is you corrupted the Lighthouse scene and created the Martin County evidence. He still claims you're protecting your partner."

"Protecting?" The detective chuckles, walking to the flowers. "Cap, is this accusation on tape?"

"I see nothing funny." The senior officer spins around, sputtering. "Absolutely nothing funny about this, Lieu..."

Fox hugs his boss.

"You've lost your damn mind." Cap stands stiffly, unable to move. "What's wrong with you?"

"We've won. This orchid is like a purple spaceship." Fox walks to the display. "How does anyone in Watters' circle have any info about the Tick DNA? Or anything to do with Tick? We've studiously contained the evidence pertaining to him. Charlie controlled all access. You're tired and emotional, fogging your memory. Let me talk to Watters."

"I *am* exhausted. I'm getting too old for days without sleep. No, not you, Fox, sorry. You can't interview Watters. Not me, either." Cap sighs. "Stan. This is all going to end up his, anyway."

"Stan? Of course, yes. You're right. Let's sew this up. And go find Dalia."

"You're a dreamer. Dalia is gone, friend."

"I live in the moment, Cap. The moment."

"I'm Stan Baskins, FBI out of Miami." Stan smiles at his notebook as he walks into the interview room. "Chief, it looks like we have a lot of problems."

"Your Palm Beach dirty cops have the problem." Watters sits, arms crossed.

"Let me talk, Jamie." The lawyer urges his client. "I'm Clive Kissock. Attorney representing Mr. Watters."

"Chief Watters!" Jamie turns sideways in his seat and glares at his attorney.

"Chief. Why don't you explain your concerns?" Stan signals the IT room. "I'm Stan Baskins, FBI, and this interview

The Sweater Case

is of Chief Jamie Watters, Inlet Colony Police, questioning a meth distribution operation in Jupiter, Florida."

"Concerning corrupt deputies out of Palm Beach, running drugs! I protect a very important village. The leaders in south Florida. They trust me."

"Yes, Chief Watters. Why don't you explain your evidence to me?" Stan sits down and leans forward. "Help me understand."

"That detective, Argall. Spoiled. Used to being protected by everyone. Everyone kowtows to the guy." Jamie squints. "Weird eyes. He scares too many people, but not me. His partner, his crony, John Tickman. All the evidence pointed to him in the murder."

"Can you describe the evidence? I need details, Chief, if I can get to corruption."

"Argall's sergeant. His military award was literally on the Lighthouse scene! His DNA is all over the place. A drug-addled call girl Harris was—whatever he was doing with her. Tickman's license was on her body. What more do you need?"

"A bit more would help. Where was the Sergeant's DNA found at the Inlet Light?"

"On the award, I told you." Watters swallows hard. "Plus, the freak Argall planted evidence in Martin county to suggest the original crime scene was miles away."

"So, your evidence is Sergeant Tickman planted his own military award at the Lighthouse? Or Dr. Argall planted it? Help me with this one."

"Well, no. Well, one of Argall's crew obviously felt bad about their corruption. At least one of his gang wanted to point the clean cops in the right direction. Probably terrified they'd be scapegoated. The Palm Beach sheriff shouldn't have answered the scene. Jupiter Police jurisdiction. Ask yourself this, Agent. Why was Argall at the scene?"

"'His crew'? Fox Argall has a crew?" Stan has to look away.

"Dr. Argall manipulated the material he found at the Martin county sheriff's?"

"Exactly! His own evidence. Now you begin to see." Watters smiles, pleased.

"I do see. Now, help me with the chain of evidence. How did you come into the knowledge of the forensics from the two scenes?"

Watters shuffles in his chair. "Well, Agent Baskins, I'm a well-respected local police officer. A leader. We have contacts. Relationships."

"Shame to reveal the magic?" Stan smiles, looking directly at the lawyer, canting his head to Watters. "I'm afraid I must insist. How do you have knowledge of this evidence?"

The lawyer leans into Watters, whispering.

"I can't reveal my contacts," Watters stammers. "I'd put them in danger."

"Danger," Stan says softly. "Chief Watters, where is Dalia Roberts being kept? I have evidence of kidnapping and murder during a kidnapping. I'll bring federal charges, and we'll demand the evidence you allege. If you're lying to a federal officer, I'll bring those charges as well. You're in an untenable position. Tell me where to find Dalia. Is she alive?"

Watters clears his throat and starts to object, but his attorney puts his arm across his client.

"Let me talk with Chief Watters, Agent Baskins. Give us a few minutes off the tape."

"So, we divvy up the bad guys?" Stan says, standing in Cap's office. "Your orchids are famous, of course, but I have to tell you, this display is more than I imagined."

"I'm not the lawyer here, but it's all federal from where I sit. Deanna's murder, that was Fuzzy Whalin. Dalia's disappearance, also Whalin according to Watters, Carley, and Morgan. They all separately described our drug magnate carting Dalia out of Harris' house. A trifecta of imperfecta." Cap measures water in his long-necked silver pitcher.

"So, it's all mine."

"All yours." Cap exhales. "We'll pick up any accessory to murder you don't want."

"What about this Alexi guy?" Stan slides down in his chair. "I want this day to be over."

"The mysterious Alexi is proclaimed by all to be uninvolved and out of the loop. Odd, that," Cap sighs. "I'm dubious, but what can we do with zero evidence? I'll look into it myself. The rest is drugs at your level, Stan. We can fight about the murder if you want. Just promise me you go after the U.S. Congressman first. Major feather for you."

"I lose some control over VIPs, Cap, but my boss is not a fan of blinking under DC pressure and this thing is broad and deep. I'd like to prove the Homeland Security connection, but who would ever talk? What does the lawyer think?" They turn to Fox.

He's slumped in one of Cap's leather chairs, sound asleep.

thirty-seven
this mad love (i would die for you)

THE CLOCK READS 2:30 a.m., but Grace isn't asleep. She hasn't been able to sleep since she came home from the hospital. Nothing helps.

Fox demanded they stay in the spare room upstairs until this case was closed. She refused, knowing her sleep difficulties would flare in a strange room.

Am I reacting... hearing the deputies in the kitchen? She sits up and straightens the covers for the twentieth time. *Where is Fox?* She doesn't even know if he's in the state.

Minutes later, the garage door opens. A familiar murmuring floats through the wall as Fox talks to the officers who sit in her kitchen. She listens as his steps move toward her. In a perverse panic, Grace wishes her husband of thirty years miles away, not walking down their hallway.

Fox opens the bedroom door, and she sees him throw his jacket on the couch at the end of the master bed. He fusses to remove his sidearm, putting the weapon in the bedside chest. *Why didn't he lock it in the gun safe? With Theiss upstairs?*

Her husband lowers himself into the flowered chair by the window.

He hates that chair. His first reaction runs through her mind.

―――

"This is not a chair, Gracie. At least, not a real chair. Not an adult chair. Your husband is over six feet tall and this chair is made for a child."

"But this fabric is lovely, Lad! We'll put it by the window."

―――

She's never seen him sit in The Kid Chair. He's crammed into the seat awkwardly, his head in his hands.

It's too small. Why do I always buy furniture he hates?

"Fox." Even as she says it aloud, the name sounds harsh to her ears. Why didn't she call him 'Lad?' She's hit with another wash of panic.

"I'm sorry, pet. I shouldn't have come in here. I'm going to go sit with the kids in the kitchen."

"Lad." She forces the endearment. Fox reacts to the strain in her voice, looking up and twisting his head to the side like he does. *Am I imagining the hurt in his eyes through the darkness?*

"Gracie?" His lilt is heavy.

He's exhausted. "Why don't you come here, lay beside me." *Don't come.*

"I'm not good company tonight." Faded light throws a shadow over his carved, high cheekbones.

"Since when has that stopped us?" The line sounds like a joke.

Fox exhales; his breath a tornado in the still room. "You're right, of course, you're right."

He's capitulating. He doesn't want to come to me. Grace's

heart sinks, and nausea floods her. In their three decades, she always builds the barriers. Sets the limits. Ellis Argall has pursued her with an unremitting passion since he first set eyes on her. *Was he only fifteen, that first day in Columbus?*

"Am I a compromise, now? A chore?" She can't keep the fear away, and fear becomes an irritation.

Fox's gaze is far away. One she has seen a thousand times, ten thousand, but never directed at her. He doesn't answer. Instead, he goes into the bathroom.

Adrenaline bursts in Grace's chest. The bathroom shower starts. She rolls over, and tears flow, wetting her pillow.

When the shower finally stops, minutes pass in silence.

What's he doing?

She slips out of bed and into the bathroom. Fox leans back on the seat in the shower. He had the high seat put in years ago when he was shot in his thigh, near his knee. He couldn't bend to sit on a normal-sized shower chair. Or get back up.

He's exhausted. Memories invade her. *His life is too difficult. He's so gifted but so... lonely. He puts up with bad treatment from others who can't or don't want to understand him.*

Including me.

"I'm sorry, sweet Lad. I'm so sorry." She bursts into tears. Real crying, the ugly kind.

Fox startles and struggles to re-orient himself. His panic would have made her cry if she wasn't crying already. He turns and puts his arms up on the tile over the shower seat, dripping water, his chin dropped on his chest.

She sees him fighting what he calls his 'Black Hole.' Her husband shivers and shuffles as he descends into dark confusion. A place she recognizes. "Lad."

"My Gracie! Oh, *carid, bendigedig melys.*" [Sweet, wonderful love.] His voice is swallowed in his pain.

Sobbing harder, she can't find her words. "You sat in The Kid Chair. My hair is gray."

The Sweater Case

"Your hair isn't very gray," he mumbles, uncertainty filling his eyes. "The Kid Chair is by the window."

"Lad."

He slides to the shower floor. "Oh, Gracie. Dalia's almost certainly dead. A drug thug took her, and we can't find her body. She's buried on a farm in rural Georgia, or tossed in the Loxahatchee swamp. I haven't told Tick yet."

Finally, her husband's distress pulls Grace through her own fears. Climbing in the shower, she drops to the wet floor, holding him. "I'm so sorry you're struggling. I'm sorry about this terrible time."

"I *am* struggling, Gracie. I'm failing. Falling. I can't do anything right anymore. I can't protect you. Can't protect Marley, or Theiss. We lost Josh. Tick is in a mess. We lost Dalia. The world's full of awful people and I attract violence like a magnet."

She lays her head on his wet, crazy curly hair as he repeats his father's condemning words. "You're a police officer, Lad. You run in, as others run out. Literally in the job description. I admire you, I adore you."

"There's no life for me without you. I would die for you, for this maddening love. I've been given such a blessing. Others live a lifetime without it. Yet I'm always one step from falling off the cliff." Tears stream down his face.

"I'll follow you off the cliff, my Ladislaw. I'll always be with you, wherever you go."

"That's the problem, my Gracie. I always take others with me."

thirty-eight
the shower seat, redux

"I'LL NEVER THINK of our shower seat exactly the same way." Fox snuggles against Grace. "Who knew?"

Soft, pink light is coming through the slats on the window blinds.

He sits up, then lays back down, pulling at the surrounding blankets. "I'm going to freeze in here. No way to treat your devoted servant." He pushes back up against her. "You're my private heat source. Like a little sun."

"We needed to replace those bad memories from the gunshot with delightful ones. I wonder, though." Grace rubs her hand over her husband's shoulders. "You're cold."

"Wonder? What wonder? As I recall, I was particularly—well—if I must say so myself, particularly wondrous last night. This morning."

"You might not have to say so yourself if you gave anyone else the chance." Grace's tinkle fairy laugh echoes in the shadows. "You were, of course, as you say, magnificent. But I wonder, why did it take us so long to notice our shower chair's height? Positioning? It's been staring us in the face for three years. Are we... Creative enough?"

Fox leans over his wife. "Creative enough?" He sputters. "Creative—"

"Now, Lad, you're violating Rule Number One. I'm questioning my role in all of this, as your wife and primary lover."

"Primary lover? This is going downhill."

"Again, I mean primary as in holding primacy."

"You're the only one holding anything of mine. I may be offended. Outraged."

"Back to creative—"

Fox throws himself sideways on the bed. "Please. Continue about creative. Talk as much as you'd like as I shrivel and freeze over here."

"Here, take my covers." Grace pokes her blankets over her husband. "I mean, sweet and Obviously Powerful Ladislaw, it took us three years to recognize the opportunities with our shower seat. What about our innovative... Instincts? Are you ever bored?"

"Bored by you? By us? How boring can we be if our daughter thinks we act like rabbits?" Fox pulls his wife over on him. "Gracie, my love. Pet, nothing—not a single, solitary thing about you is boring."

"I want to be a hiding place for you. An oasis."

He squeezes her tighter against him. "I'm the one," he whispers. "I want to look in your eyes as I love you. I want to hold you face-to-face, your sweet nose pressed on mine. I don't need or want 'creativity' in our time together. I want to be so close to you, I can absorb you. Becoming one with you is a sacred thing. The only way to reach beyond my failing ability outside this lovely space. It's not a physical carnival act."

Grace buries her face in Fox's chest. "Last night, before, when we had the—spat."

"I'd call it nothing more than a squabble."

"The Squabble, then. It hit me how unfair it is to you. I put so much on you. Is it your duty to control other intelligent adults? I blame you, sometimes, for what others do. Like Roofie and Tick. Stel did, too, at the Pretend Authentic Cuban party."

Fox narrows his eyes, and she kisses him, continuing. "I warned, scolded. I scolded you about the guys going to Detroit like they were children or puppets when Roof and Tick are full-grown men with their own minds. Stel blamed you. Cap blamed you. The Detroit Lark is only one example. My eyes suddenly opened last night, and you were so tired and sad, squeezed into The Kid Chair. You carry too much. What's not yours?"

"Ah, Gracie." Fox kisses his wife's head. "I appreciate your slightly blinkered trust in my benevolent intentions. I'm a bit Machiavellian, to be perfectly fair."

thirty-nine
grinding while sleep deprived

THE SUN IS BARELY UP, but humidity already forms heavy streaks of condensation on the Argall's windows.

Tick sits bolt upright at the antique walnut kitchen table, rolling his shoulders. He's whooshing out paced breaths. *One muscle at a time.*

Stan's head is laid in his folded arms, and he's snoring.

The deputies assigned to protect the Argall family lean on the granite counters, drinking the expensive coffee Tick bought for Fox. A crumpled, empty bag is on the counter, surrounded by a couple of stray beans.

And the grinder. The grinder is filthy. "The coffee wasn't for you," Tick snarls. "Clean up after yourselves."

The older officer puts the grinder in the sink but folds both hands possessively over the steaming mug. "It's freezing in here. I need gloves."

"Ticker," Fox soothes. He glides into the bright room, finishing the knot on his tie. "What're you growling about?"

"My coffee's gone." The sergeant frowns and adjusts himself on the walnut chair. His legs hunch up toward his chin.

"You're in danger of crushing my wife's delicate furniture."

"Your new grinder, Shay. Ah, man. Coffee, better coffee beans..." Tick glares at the deputies. "Better beans contain oil. If uncleaned, oil remains in the grinder, jamming up the grind. Occasional cleaning, it's all I ask."

"Reasonable, right, boys?" Fox smiles and tilts his head at his grouchy partner.

Tick throws up his hands. "What kind of fu... freaking chair is this? Is this Theiss' playhouse table and chairs? This can *not* be an actual adult dining set."

"Right?" Fox reaches into a high cabinet shelf. "Gracie just bought it. Ticker, come here. I hid this bag, apparently where I can't reach it. Luckily, there's a semi-giant on our team. Over here. Come, come."

"Now we're in a hurry. You're the only one who got any sleep."

Fox glances up at the officers, who refuse to meet his eyes. "Well, I'm always in a hurry for hot coffee. Gracie has the A/C at 68 degrees. Haven't you noticed? Your wonderful, warm coffee. Plus, I need the caffeine. I'm older."

"Not too old," observes the youngest uniform, without looking up.

Tick glares at the deputy, missing the implication. "Dr. Argall is certainly not too old."

"The master bathroom's right behind this wall." Stan yawns, stretching his arms up and pointing. "Florida-level insulation. Thin to non-existent. Noise carries."

"The master bath?" Tick scowls and motions down the hall. "The deputies can use the guest bath, Agent Baskins."

"My sergeant makes the best coffee," Fox interrupts. "I wouldn't want to adulterate your fancy brew. Come, make us all a pot."

"Need to wash the grinder first." Tick waves the officers

out of the way. "You guys go sit in the yard. We live in south Florida. Go warm yourselves outside. Thank your stars you're not hunkered in North Dakota. Go sniff a flower or something."

Stan motions Fox to the living room. "We've got loose ends. I hate loose ends. Tell Tick about Dalia right now. Cap will call you guys any minute."

Tick leans against the door frame. "Cap called me at 2 a.m. last night."

Face falling, Fox sighs. "Ticker, I'm chuffed. I planned to tell you this morning when we found time to talk."

"Yeah, you're famous for 'talking' and shit. Such a comforting guy." His partner's green eyes flash, but Tick chuckles. "Oh, don't give me those hurt kitten blinks. Let's talk about something more important than your fragile feelings. I'm thinking deeply about this situation. I've got an idea."

"Deeply? Thinking deeply, what does that even mean?" The detective moans. "I'm too tired for this new grammar."

Stan closes his eyes, exasperated. "If we are on some Fox and Tick Show tangent..."

Patting the FBI agent on the chest, Tick interrupts. "Isn't there a Bat Signal, or some way to call for your Natalie chick?"

Fox's mouth twists, and he stares. "Bat Signal? My Natalie chick?"

"It's early, guys," Stan interjects. "Bad stuff happened kind of non-stop, and none of us have slept."

"Some less than others," Fox mumbles.

Stan pushes through. "Can we all speak English plainly? Tick, are you referring to 'Shut Down the Turnpike' Natalie?"

"What?" Tick swings around on his partner, his voice rising. "What the hell? Shut down the turnpike?"

"Just the restroom, Ticker. No need to..."

"Wait!" Stan raises his voice. "Stop. One person talks at a time. I can't follow your partner-shorthand-interrupting thing."

"Stan never raises his voice," Fox warns. "He's preternaturally calm, for a cop."

"I want to hear about the freaking turnpike." Tick walks off, grousing. "After I pour myself some fu— effing coffee, dammit."

"Ticker is sensitive, even at the best of times," Fox mutters.

"I heard you, Dr. Argall. I'm not getting you coffee."

The detective walks back into the kitchen. "Stan, you better come in here to drink coffee."

"Or risk the wrath of Mom. No coffee in the living room." Marley comes down the stairs. "Hello, Stan."

"Yes, sorry if we were loud. Did we wake you? The baby?" Stan's light blond coloring can't hide the red blush.

"No," Marley stage-whispers. "You mean Dad and Tick were loud. Mostly Tick. Dad upsets him, sometimes. I'll go find Mom. Nice to see you again."

"Stan!" Tick yells. "Work to do. In here. I'll pour *you* coffee."

Marley smiles at the agent and heads down the hallway to the master suite.

"I think Natalie is key." The sergeant's voice comes from the kitchen. "What's this about the turnpike?"

Stan's gaze follows Marley as he walks into the kitchen. "Lieutenant Argall, will you explain the Turnpike Incident? Try to be comprehensive. None of us are buying any memory lapses from our resident genius."

The detective pulls his phone out of his pocket. "OK, OK." He begins a game of Brick Breaker and stops talking.

"Oh, no, Shay. You talk. When and how is Natalie Forester connected to The Sweater Case?" Tick taps the table in front of his boss. "Stan, this woman caused trouble in previous cases. She's obsessed with our fancy man, here. Goes back... how long?"

"A while." Fox grinds his jaw. "I agree. Tick, Natalie might be a service to us. She has contacts we wouldn't want but might profit from. No idea how to reach her. None. She shows up when she wants."

"I have an idea," Tick says. "We put you in the spotlight, and she will show up. That's our Bat Signal. A Fox Signal."

forty
pain, pain, everywhere

DARKNESS SWALLOWS the Argall living room as Fox crouches at his gun safe, removing the Smith and Wesson 5946. He checks the thumb safety with his left hand, and then his right, before shoving it into a ballistic vest holster. He's dressed in dark jeans, a black V-neck tee shirt, and black boots.

"Dad, where's your Glock?" Marley whispers, her voice echoing in the quiet room.

Fox blinks and exhales. "My left shoulder holster, like always."

"Can you use either firearm with either hand?"

"I prefer the Glock and my right hand. But yes, I can use both. I have a six-second delta between hands with the Glock. Nine with the S and W."

"I'll pray for you. I love you."

He drops his head as tears fill his eyes. "I love you more than I have ever been able to express."

"I know, Daddy."

The Sweater Case

Marley dials her Uncle Roofie. "Dad just left. He's in his ballistic vest and he has both of his firearms. I'm not sure what to do."

"Never mind, Marls. You called the right person. It'll be OK."

"Nothing is really OK, Uncle Roof."

The SUV bumps down the dirt road, spinning gravel as the sun colors the sky red. The headlights are off.

"Red sky in the morning, sailors take warning," Roofie says grimly.

"Faith isn't fading, is it, my brother?" Fox glances over at his oldest friend.

"When anyone lacks wisdom, let them ask for it. Warnings are blessings." Roofie puts his hand on the detective's shoulder. "We're ready for this encounter, *brawd*."

House lights appear in the distance.

"Walk up and knock, or what?" Fox steers the vehicle to the verge.

"Walk up and knock." Roofie clicks open his safety belt. "I called Fuzzy at the last rest stop."

"They say I'm hard to control." The detective slams the car door hard as he exits. An announcement.

The porch light flips on, and a massive man comes out onto the porch. He's alone.

"Edgar Allen Parks. Never thought I'd see the day." Fuzzy Whalin's deep Georgia accent booms in the rosy shadows.

"A bit far south for me, Fuzz. Figuratively, that is."

"I don't sleep as well as I used to, Edgar, but it's still early for visitors. What can I do for you?"

"I'm looking for a friend. Dalia Roberts."

Booming laughter splits the pink morning mist. "Haven't

met anyone named Dalia. But who's this I see? Who's your pretty boyfriend? Provocative to wear an Ohio State sweatshirt to my place, don't you think? Go, Bulldogs."

"The Ohio State University, mate." Fox pushes his accent hard. "*The* Ohio State."

"Ah. The famous Doctor Argall. Wondered if I'd meet you, *mate*," Fuzzy growls. "Edgar, bringing cops to my home?"

"Fox Argall, meet Fuzzy Whalin. Fox is a Palm Beach county deputy sheriff, Fuzz. Way out of his jurisdiction."

"We playin' games, now? Never was your way of doin' things, Edgar."

"No games. Fox has a personal connection to Dalia. We'd like her back, no repercussions." Roofie continues to walk toward the porch.

"None from you. All you can promise."

Roofie laughs. "You have a whole host of people wanting repercussions, but we aren't them. We have a single goal. Dalia inside our car, heading back to Florida."

"Wish I could help you for old times' sake." Fuzzy sits down in a wide rocker, and it screeches an objection at the weight. "You're claiming control, but you don't have any."

"No control necessary. For us, it's simple. Dalia. Then we leave."

A sudden gunshot blast screams from the cornfield to the right of the house, grazing Fox's shoulder.

"Down!" He yells, pulling Roofie to the wet grass. "Back to the car, fast."

Two men run out of the woods, one heading to the porch. Another gunshot from deep in the field takes the first man down. The other hits the ground, looking over at the SUV. He flattens himself, aims, and fires twice at the vehicle in fast succession.

Fox falls back against the door. "I'm hit, Roof."

A shotgun explodes from inside the house, knocking the screened door from its hinges. Fuzzy Whalin crashes to the porch, shattering boards and falling halfway through the hole. His head slams against the broken wood, blood spraying.

A slender figure stands in the open doorway behind Fuzzy's body.

It's Dalia.

"Dalia! Get down! Second shooter, get down!" Fox screams, raising his Glock to the dark figure twisting on the ground.

The second man turns and aims for Dalia. Before he can fire, a rifle shot comes from the woods, and the side of his face blows off.

She remains standing in the doorway for a minute, then slides to the ground.

Fox crawls on his elbows to the porch, waiting for the next shot.

It never comes.

"Dalia, Dalia, girl." The detective scrambles up the porch steps on his hands and knees.

"I'm here, Dr. Argall." Her voice is low but strong. "You better attend to your friend."

Roofie lies face down on the ground, next to the open door.

forty-one
all politics is local

FOX IS READING a text when Cap comes into his hospital room.

"You're pale. Pain nauseating you?" The senior officer throws a newspaper onto the sliding table pulled across the hospital bed. "Did you see this?"

"No, not the pain. This text upsets me. Good grief, Skipper. A newspaper? You're a dinosaur." Fox lays back, his eyes closed.

"Read it, Lieutenant."

The paper is local, but the headline is across a national news wire.

> *U.S. Congressional Representative from Florida*
> *Caught Up in Drug Sting*
> *Blackmail Attempt Brings Down Michael Harris*

"Well, this is interesting. Glad to hear a blackmail attempt brought him down," Fox snarks.

"We don't need the light of credit." Cap flings himself into a chair. "We need shadows."

The Sweater Case

"Told ya. Shadows are our friend."

"Hold off on the sarcasm, Dr. 'I'm a Superhero.'" Cap frowns. "Details in this report go further than our case. Two other state reps are implicated. One from Massachusetts and one from New York state."

"Real investigative reporting that's not propaganda? There's something new."

"No journalism involved. Someone unknown handed this to them, an inside scoop."

"Ah." Fox grimaces, slouching in the bed. "Bullets hurt. So who handed it to them?"

"I think we both have suspicions. We have to talk about this. I'm forever grateful Roofie made it through the surgery. Dalia is home and safe. But dammit all. Why were you and Roofie in Gwinnett? I mean, together?"

"Roof knew Fuzzy from way back. We had one limited chance to rescue Dalia." Fox's eyes are down, and he flips his phone over. "I had to take the chance."

"Fox. We're a hell-bonded team, you and me. Georgia authorities are grateful. Fuzzy Whalin's gone. He was so powerful, no one can replace him. The network will move out of Georgia's backyard. They have dozens of crime scenes. I did my job and made sure we're skating in it all. I've assured no bitching. Georgia has jurisdiction and gets all the credit, plus Charlie's on borrow to lead the forensics. What will they find?"

Fox frowns. "Three groups of shooters. The two men who shot me and Roofie. I think they were covering Fuzzy."

"They missed their assignment."

"This brings us to Dalia, the second shooter. She obviously came at Whalin from behind. I think there were two shooters in the second group. The third team was in the woods, watching the watchers."

"To the ruin of the watchers," Cap sighs. "We have three dead bad guys. So we're missing at least two more?"

"There was a third team of two. One dead-eye with a rifle, the other using a Sig. I could hear it."

"We appear to have lost the third group. We don't have the shooter with the rifle. No evidence found to date."

"I'm betting Charlie will find evidence of two missing 'bad guys,' one with the rifle, one shooting a Sig Sauer." Wriggling, Fox sits up. "Skip, I got a text. I'm sure it's from Natalie."

"Natalie? What the hell does she want? Now I'm nauseated."

The detective hands Cap his phone:

> Bank box, Gunther Bank, Highway One, Tequesta. Key in your glove box. Sig, Cwnsler.

"*Cwnsler*. She's using Welsh to prod you into a trap," Cap says. "I'll send a Hazmat team. Trace that text."

"There's no need. She's not going to hurt me. The burner she used to send this is long gone," Fox murmurs. "The note says 'Sig.' Charlie'll probably find a bullet from a Sig Sauer killed the guy who shot me. I heard a Sig."

"I can still try. How did she know you were in some damn farmland in northern Georgia?"

The detective doesn't answer. He swings his legs to the side of the bed and groans. "We'll never trace the text anywhere valuable. Someone's Aunt Martha in Peoria. You know it's a burner. I'm going to the bank."

"Get back in bed, you idiot. You're a fucking physician."

"Exactly. Hospitals are dangerous for the minimally injured. All kinds of enemy combatants, bad bacteria, out to get unsuspecting patients. Hospital bugs. I'll tell you all about nosocomial infections right after you explain orchids to me.

Help me out of here before I catch something. Take me to the bank."

The bank box lies open. Original documents of a multinational drug ring spread across the table.

Cap marvels. "What a haul. The conspiracy is facilitated by Michael Harris, U.S. Rep from Florida, and two additional PermaPoliticians who serve on the Homeland Security Committee. Emails, texts, travel docs, and bank information outline the state and federal representatives who are involved. The entire criminal enterprise started with a group of five, all of whom went to a fancy university in Massachusetts."

"See?" Fox says. "Hence, I rejected those nasty Ivy League schools for Ohio State."

"Natalie sent all this evidence?" Cap shakes his head.

"Did she? We're not even sure she told me where to find it." Fox sighs. "No one will find any evidence of her. We can give her to the Feds, and they'll scrap with her. She'd enjoy it. But why? We know nothing. If she's involved, she was on our side. This time."

"This time," Cap repeats. "You think Natalie put a team in the woods? Watching the watchers?"

"Her team? No, not directly. She's the Chess Master, Cap. Mercenaries, no doubt. We won't see her fingerprints. Crikey. Stan's going to be chaffed, isn't he?"

"You just considered your federal pawn, Dr. Argall? I can tell you he's already pissed. Be ready for it."

"Never a pawn, Cap. A knight. My horseman. Why can't we give these documents to him? No explanations. You were the one who said it: stay in the shadows."

"Fucking incapable of anything but finagling, Fox. Machiavellian at your very core."

"Thanks, Cap. It's a treasure hunt. Fun when the pieces come together."

"Machiavelli was a villain, Lieutenant. It wasn't a compliment."

The detective chuckles. "It's about perspective. The thin line of villain and hero depends on where you stand, *hen ffrind*."

forty-two
epilogue is prologue

"GIVE HER TIME, TICKER." Fox is playing Brick Breaker at his new kitchen table. "She's had several severe traumas. There are too many people here. Chaotic."

"Seven people are here, not counting Theiss. Three of them are your family."

"Everyone here is family, how does that mitigate the chaos?"

Piano music flows into the kitchen from the living room, warmed by a Thanksgiving turkey roasting in the oven. Marley's playing 'Rebel Heart'. She sings softly, and the deep contralto fills the house.

Tick stands next to the kitchen window, looking out at Dalia, who is sitting in the Argalls' backyard with Roofie, Stella, and Grace. Theiss plays in her new sandbox. "She came for Roofie. Or worse, for you. Not for me. Did you see her face when she saw me? Like she'd been struck."

Fox furrows his brows at the young sergeant. "Rule Number One, *consigliere*. Nothing is remotely about you."

"Exactly," Tick growls.

The detective puts his phone on the kitchen table. "Come here, Tick. Sit with me."

"At least I can sit in this new chair."

"Right?" Fox pats the large padded chair beside him. "See what Gracie did for you? She bought a new kitchen table set. Suitable for semi-giants. Come."

Tick throws himself in the chair. "Comfortable," he grumbles.

"All for you, because you're my wife's breakfast boyfriend."

"Your wife is a perfect person. Marley's really talented."

"Yes." Pain flashes through his narrowed eyes. "Marley's remarkable. Let's talk about relationships, John."

"Uh, boss. Relationships? I'm dubious of this subject as a discussion between us."

"Ah." Fox glances down. "True. My struggle with relationships. I fail in this because I value my own ideas above others, not because I don't love others. I love. Frankly, I love with desperation. I'm convinced I know better and so, to love and protect, I sometimes ignore respect."

"Sometimes, Shay?"

"OK, often. Mostly."

Marley begins to play 'It's Inevitable.'

"Here's the thing, Tick. Dalia's sister fell apart at some point, right? Her twin. A drug addict and mule. And what else?" Fox's voice drops to a whisper. "We can imagine too much of the 'else.' Her only family, Ticker. Then, in the middle of a crazy shambles, her twin is shot, and she reacted."

"She was desperate."

"Yes. I may not understand relationships, but I understand desperation. Dalia broke her sister's sternum in her desperation. It takes a lot of pressure to break a sternum through. The blood work shows she was attempting CPR for a while. Probably as Fuzzy, if not others, laughed. Get in her head and heart a bit."

Marley steps into the kitchen. She sags against the refrigerator. Her eyes are bloodshot, with dark hollows underneath. "I examined the body, Tick. 'Desperation' may not reach it. Dalia was out of control."

"Then, was she forced to watch the desecration to her sister's lip?" Tick exhales and lays back in his chair.

"And, when people you love die in front of you, and you're a medical professional, and supposed to save them—" Marley chokes. She turns to go back into the living room, then she stops. "Dad, I'm leaving medicine."

"Marley!" Tick stands up.

Fox puts his hand on his sergeant. "I understand, Marls. You didn't consider it lightly. Maybe we can talk, your Mom and me, with you? I should tell you a few things."

The back door opens, and Cap sticks his head in. Tick startles. "Oh, it's you."

"Thanks, Sergeant. Bordering on disrespect for a senior officer, but as it's Thanksgiving, I'll let it slide." Cap takes in the scene. "Sarah and I dropped in on the way north. Come, toast with us before we leave."

Fox picks up his phone and follows Cap without looking at Marley.

"Marley, I'm so sorry about Josh," Tick stammers. He starts toward her and hesitates.

"We've all struggled. It's been a bit beyond." Marley joins the big man, stretching her arm around his waist. "Argalls love an understatement."

In the yard, Cap pours glass after glass of Blanton's bourbon. "No, everyone must have a glass. I never said this out loud, but Kentucky bourbon is almost equal to spirits from my Scotland."

"It's as expensive," Fox mutters. "My last bottle. Blanton's is hard to find."

"Santa Claus will restock your coffers." Grace smiles.

Cap clears his throat and raises his glass. "Roofie, while

your lovely wife, Stella, and I object to your methods, I thank you—and the always objectionable Dr. Argall—for saving our Dalia. Here's to our own Bravehearts, *salut*."

The group drinks, an awkward silence filling the backyard.

"What did I miss? Please don't tell me I missed bourbon." Beth Wilson throws the gate open into the backyard from the alley, followed by a second woman.

"Alvie! Beth." Grace runs to the women. "Alvie, I'm so glad you made it!"

"I wouldn't miss an Argall dinner," Alvie says. "That would just be stupid."

Turning to her guests, Grace says, "You know Beth. This is my first cousin, Alvie Dawes. We were raised together in southeastern Ohio. She's more my sister. My busy little sister, who lives in DC now. Alvie's a busy biopharmaceutical executive."

Alvie laughs. "Hardly, Gracie Moe. More like a BioPharm Peon. And I'm moving to Boca."

"Boca! Right here!" Grace claps her hands.

Roofie catches Fox's eye and motions him over. "Help your old friend. Tick, I need both of you. Take me in the house, mind? I want to walk. Legs cramping."

The two men lift Roofie out of the wheelchair and head to the kitchen.

Inside the kitchen, the pastor says, "Boys, we need to keep the Fox Signal to ourselves. Agreed? Ellis, you underestimate Natalie Forester. The woman can't be trusted."

"She almost certainly saved your life, my brother."

"Nonsense. You would have saved me." Roofie groans. "Careful on my bad side, Tick. Those shooters just didn't give you time."

"I would have tried, but I wasn't aware you were down. No, Roof, I believe Natalie sent the second team into the woods and the field. I know it. Your visit to Ann Carley saved our hides."

"What about Ann Carley? What will she say about all this?" Tick looks nauseated. "Will she mention Roofie's visit? What will she say about Natalie to the FBI? The DA?"

"Talk? Nah, Ticker," Fox says. "Roofie visited her in a pastoral role and vaguely mentioned the trip to north Georgia. Everyone knows we went, no secret there. Ann won't mention Natalie. She's in thrall to her sister, and likely terrified. Or adores her."

"Or both. Talk about complicated," Roofie says. "She passed the message perfectly, regardless. And here we stand, mostly in one piece."

forty-three
the sweater case is sewn up

BLACK FRIDAY after Thanksgiving

Stan, Cap, and Fox sit at the senior officer's round table, drinking coffee and eating Missy's cookies.

"Tick took the day off to do what?" Cap asks.

"Take Dalia and his mother to some retail sale or something." Fox shakes his head. "Naff."

Stan Baskins smiles. "Tell me how this Sweater Case came together, people. Leave Tick alone. The poor guy has been through it. I assume you're healing nicely, Dr. Argall?"

He doesn't answer, his head down in his game.

"OK, I'll go first," Cap says. "Our favorite asshole is fine. A tiny graze under his arm. Fuzzy Whalin drove the entire enterprise. He terrified the whole corrupt crew. Michael Harris thought he was in charge, but stepped into a swamp with a snake he never dreamed existed."

"Lost control before he ever had it, the poncey wanker," Fox murmurs.

"My lieutenant has selective hearing," Cap says. "Harris set up the Mexico deal, then Fuzzy showed up at Harris' home. Demanded expansion into other parts of South America. Alexi had the receipts on everything."

"The same Alexi who was bizarrely out of the loop. It appears the butler was utterly innocent." Fox interjects. "Still not buying it."

"So, let me get this straight," Stan says. "Fuzzy shows up at Harris' house with the twins. He threatens to blackmail Harris with Deanna, his drug mule mistress. Fuzzy demands the current drug action and demands expansion from Mexico to Columbia. A physical fight occurs, and Whalin shoots Deanna."

Cap nods. "After Deanna was shot, Dalia tried to revive her. We know how that went."

"Then, the Jupiter cop — Guy Morgan — dragged the body to the Lighthouse and contrived the entire scene?" Stan asks.

"Yes, but he couldn't move the body up the stairs. Not on his own." Fox mumbles as he plays his game. "Dalia was in the room as Jamie Watters and Morgan got into a fight about who would remove the body."

"Then Watters and Michael Harris decided to use the Lighthouse, but Watters refused to help Morgan and the body was too difficult to move up the stairs." Cap pours himself more coffee. "They left a single body part instead. Dalia watched them cut off her sister's lip."

"I'm confused about the fresh blood and Tick's military award," Stan says. "Surely, the details weren't decided in the moment?"

Fox stretches his legs out and groans. "No, a bit later, I suspect. They still had a body to dispose of, and Morgan got too cute. He and Ann Carley were dating. He naturally went to her for help with the body."

"Those lunatics contrived to frame Tick. Deanna's imported handmade Mexican sweater had been torn in two in the melee. Someone threw half of it in the ditch. The exact wrong ditch, as it turns out. It ran alongside a property owned by a farmer furious about the clogged ditches who took the sweater to the Martin county sheriff."

"Neither Carley nor Morgan could have known Fox was going to show up and see blood on a small piece of red sweater." Stan chuckles.

"His weirdo sense of smell caught the methamphetamine."

Fox squirms in his seat, and stands up, walking to the window. "The next part is a guess. Carley mentions the crazy over-educated detective to her sister."

"'Turnpike Natalie Forester.'" Stan laughs again. "What a shit show."

"Turnpike? What?" Cap wheels on his lieutenant. "What?"

Fox moans, banging his forehead on the blinds. "It was only the restroom. Not 'The Turnpike.' So dramatic, good grief."

"Never mind. I don't care." The captain snarls, going to his orchids. "I do *not* fucking care."

Stan lays his head back. "You guys are entertaining, I'll admit. OK, just finish with the blood. And Tick."

Cap continues. "Our guess is Carley tells Natalie about meeting Fox, which was the same day as the craziness at Harris' house. Asked her for help about disposing of the body. Who knows? Natalie, who's always been bitchy about Tick, decides it's funny to implicate him. Tick still doesn't know how they got the award ribbon or the outdated license. They were in his drawer in his apartment."

"The blood was Deanna's. Morgan and Carley drained the blood and tossed it on the scene. Then they threw the body out at the Jackson ER." Fox finishes his game and puts his phone in his pocket.

"And I get the drug scheme corruption documents," Stan

says. "As a consolation prize for being manipulated and used by my friend."

"Quite a consolation. Five sitting politicians? It's a first-class present." Fox frowns. "Oh. Cap. I'm taking a leave of absence. Grace's cousin — you met her at Thanksgiving? Alvie is in some kind of trouble and needs an attorney with expertise in healthcare. Seems she's a reluctant whistleblower. I'm sure you guys will be fine for a few days."

coming soon! the reluctant whistleblower

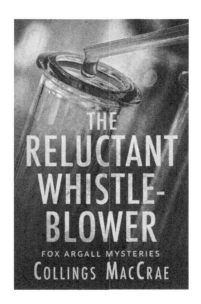

Prologue

The Inlet, Boca Raton, Florida, Pre-dawn
 The splash sends a dozen birds flying, driving the fish into the black depths of the brackish water. The custom-tailored

shirt, smeared yellow from the streetlight, flutters and slowly sinks into the fading darkness. A burnished, Italian-made leather shoe rolls to the surface, rights itself, and bobs like a tiny boat in the returning calm.

"Whatever made that splash is huge. It has to be an alligator," a voice warns. "C'mon, move back across the road, away from the water."

"No 'gator's going after an adult jogging past," a second voice teases. "Alligator paranoia in south Florida."

Chapter One: Qui What?
Las Vegas, Nevada, National Sales Meeting, Phaelon Pharmaceuticals

"Are you threatening me?" Alvie Dawes leans her six-foot frame into the diminutive George Cabelli's personal space, forcing him onto the metal bench. "Right here, in this very public place?"

Her voice carries into the glistening lobby of the Vegas casino, and several heads turn to listen.

Caballi squirms and scoots further away from his colleague. "I'm saying if you don't change some of your current vocal concerns, you'll experience a consequence you won't enjoy."

"Let's be clear here. As Phaelon's Human Resources lawyer, you say the company intends to fire me for doing my job?"

The attorney flinches. "As your friend, Alvie, I say you're in danger of being fired."

"And I get a say, too. As *your friend*, you need to explain facts to someone higher in the company. Firing me won't solve your problem. And you *have* a problem. Significant problems, in fact."

"Can we lower our voices?"

Alvie sweeps her hand toward a hotel entrance swathed in Christmas decorations. Groups hover behind brightly colored lights, pretending not to watch the pair.

"So, friend. You prepared this 'private' talk to warn me, smack in the pathway to the meeting rooms? Tantalizingly adjacent to the famous holiday light extravaganza?"

"I want you to take me seriously."

"Oh, I see you're serious. So do two dozen of our colleagues, scattered here and there in tittering bunches. Did you plan the visual? Let me add to your drama." She bends to put her face in his. "Tell our other upper-echelon *friends* to do what they need to do. I'm going to continue to tell the truth. I'll do my job until I don't have one anymore."

"Alvie, just drop everything. Take a few days off, calm down."

"Did you just tell me to calm down?" She drops to the seat beside him. "Re-direct your advice, Counselor. Phaelon is foundering in a failed new product launch, and your Immunology Group sales director threatened a company revenue recognition accountant to 'make sure the right numbers are reported' at the end of the quarter. He demanded she report accrued revenue as cash income. Patently illegal. You have a Vice President who told my boss at a company meeting to—and I quote—'Get your *C-word* under control.' He called me the C-word."

"None of your facts matter, Alvie. You're the target. I'm warning you as your friend."

"Warning received. Now, I have a presentation to give. Wonder who'll come to the show?"

George presses his lips white and swallows hard.

"Not joining me? Too bad."

Coming Soon! The Reluctant Whistleblower

Boca Raton, Florida, A Week Later

Grace Argall pats her cousin's hand. "Alvie, sweetie. Talk to Fox. He can help you think through these things with your company. You've got too good a gut to ignore anything."

"I only bring the issues to you as my favorite bioethicist." Alvie collapses on a bronze leather chair and a half, pulling her cousin beside her. "You hold the PhD in bioethics. Your husband—you call him Fox now—it's no good. He's still Ellis to me, I just can't call him Fox."

"He answers to a lot of names," Grace giggles.

"More than anyone else I know. Anyway, he's a Palm Beach detective. And I'm not sure what concerns me about Phaelon. Just some weirdness. He'll drill me and I've got no answers."

"He will *not* drill you. That's silly! Fox may be in law enforcement now, but he was a healthcare attorney for years. He's a physician and trained as a researcher. A bit more than a detective. He can help you think through."

Alvie sighs. "I don't mean... of course. I don't want to drag him into something that's probably nothing. Gracie-girl, tell me how Marley and Theiss are doing since the accident. They're far more important than my chaotic life."

Grace's blue eyes darken and fill with tears. "Josh's death has us all in a tailspin. Marley most, of course. Theiss is confused and wanders the rooms calling for her daddy. Marls recoils every time, and fights to settle her."

"Living with you is a blessing for them."

"Josh's parents are such a great support for them, too, through their own devastating pain. They put our girls first."

Alvie hugs her cousin tight. "How's Ellis handling it all?"

"Not well, understandably. He and Marley struggle so. They're peas in a pod. Neither can see they're exactly alike."

"Not exactly alike." Alvie raises in the chair and rests her elbows on her knees. "I'm just going to say it out loud. Ellis focuses on you and the door clangs shut and locks."

"Focuses on me." Grace rubs her forehead and sighs. "Yes."

"The focus closes others out, Gracie May. Closes Marley out."

The TV blares in the background.

"WARNING. This is a weather warning. A storm capable of high winds and significant amounts of rainfall is entering the area now and is expected to remain dangerous for the next 24 hours. Please do not drive on the roads and find shelter immediately."

"Speaking of your husband," Alvie says, "he better arrive soon. The weather people predicted this storm will be worse here at the lake."

"I'll call him. I've no idea where he is."

"Tell him to stop and get my pizza from Papa Boo's."

"Fox hates delivery pizza," Grace smiles. "You ask for pizza and a lecture is coming."

Alvie snarls and twirls, sticking out her butt. "I'm not afraid of your husband."

Grace giggles as her phone rings. "Speaking of my great love. Lad, you're on speaker. Where are you? The storm's coming. Head back to Alvie's, pronto, or be stuck who-knows-where."

"I'm minutes away. Maybe twenty."

"Great! Drop by Boo's and pick up a pizza for Alvie. She's called it in."

"Pizza? Gracie, delivery pizza?" Fox groans.

"Nutritional lecture coming from Dr. Argall? How fun!" Alvie yells.

"This pizza is *not* the best choice, cousin." The wind howls through the phone. "I think only of you."

"Yeah, Ellis, whatever," Alvie says. "Boo's pizza is the closest thing to heaven. Your scorn is misplaced. The order is under 'Alvie' and paid for. Hold the box. Never have to touch the pie; no contributing to my delinquency with your wallet."

"Delivery pizza is gross and a health risk," Fox objects. "Not only a nutritional lecture. An infectious disease lecture. Eating a delivery pizza is like shaking hands with a dozen teenagers and licking your fingers."

"Pssh, Ellis Argall. Pizza is a delicacy."

"Are you challenging my credentials?"

"Yes, I think it *was* a challenge, Lad." Grace giggles again. "Love you. Hurry! You're too cute to wash away. Bye, baby." She disconnects the call.

"You still call him 'Lad.' How sickening." Alvie pokes her cousin in her side. "The fabulous love story of Dorothea and Ladislaw. I need to read the novel."

"Nana would be so disappointed you haven't already. Middlemarch is her favorite book." Grace hugs her cousin again. "He'll be here soon. Talk your work issues through with us. I hate seeing you so confused. You have a deep crease between your eyebrows."

"I *am* conflicted. I feel hot breath on my neck, but my brain keeps telling me I'm overreacting."

Chapter Two: Et Sequitur

"I'm here," Fox calls up the octagonal staircase from the first floor. "Junk food and fresh filets in tow, and just in time.

Rain's flooding down. We're in for it. Turn down the A/C, it's freezing in here. Ice is forming."

"Put on a sweatshirt," Alvie growls. "You stopped at TC Market for steak? I have food here, you nut."

"You do *not* have proper food, Alvie. All you have is processed things resembling food. I got spinach, canned tomatoes, a fresh swordfish filet for my lovely wife, a filet mignon for me, and baked bread from the bakery at TC Market. My Gracie is a miracle worker with actual food. I also got your pizza — with some trepidation."

Alvie shoves the tall, oddly feline man. "Not everyone can be an intellectual prodigy and a nutritionist. You're the exception."

"Yes. Sad, that." Fox pushes his Welsh accent, kissing his cousin on the cheek.

"Honey, Alvie has a work thing." Grace calls.

"Grace Dawes Argall." Alvie throws a wadded-up napkin at her cousin. "Ignore your wife. I've got a question. More an observation. Brits always drop half the words off any sentence. Any word. Every word is eligible for the 'drop' thing. Part of grammar doesn't matter. Is it boredom, halfway through your sentence you decide to stop talking? Weird, that."

"The rain's coming down in buckets." Fox looks out the wide windows at the Inlet. "Will we lose power out here?"

"'Out here,' like we're in the woods and not in Boca Inlet." Alvie rolls her eyes.

Grace laughs. "Always on his own wavelength. We could dance naked in the middle of the room."

"No, I would notice dancing. The 'drop thing,' as you call it, is mostly adverbs. We Brits do abbreviate sentences." The detective opens and closes the blinds on the window. "What's the work issue? You're trying to distract me with sentence structure and dancing, which generally won't work. You don't seem eager to discuss your problem, Alvie."

"Not eager, because the issue or issues aren't even real yet. Or maybe ever. I don't want to drag you into anything. No spoiling the day."

"Ah. Drag me in. See Alvie's chairs, Gracie? They fit real adult humans, unlike your furniture choices. Interesting thought, yes?" He continues to roll the blinds and the room fades and brightens as thunder crashes.

"Stop messing with the light, husband, and I'll find out where Alvie buys her furniture."

"Deal." Fox drops into the blue tapestry chair and starts playing on his phone. "Alvie. You're trained in law. Give me a Statement of Facts. I'm very good at listening. I get a bad rap because I don't respond."

"The not responding thing throws people off. Add the never looking at people plus your incessant gameplay, and *voilà*. The 'bad rap' for not listening."

Fox raises his eyebrows and tilts his head, continuing to play.

"OK, here goes." Alvie slides into an oversized chair and a half, pulling her legs under her. "I had a weird conversation last week at the Phaelon Vegas meeting. Maybe a threat."

"Maybe? You don't know? Seems odd." The Brick Breaker music bops in the background. "Threat? To whom? By whom?"

"The HR attorney assigned to my department."

"Isn't he your friend? You refused dinner with me on more than one occasion to dine with him when I was in DC. Something we need to know about this yob?"

"He's not a 'yob,' Fox. The dinners were work," Alvie sighs. "The threat. It wasn't really a threat, more a warning. Set to be very public at the meeting. He chose the location to allow the widest audience possible."

"Nefarious at best. What are you doing to merit such attention?"

"That's my confusion. I'm doing nothing beyond my assigned job. Minor compliance concerns with the sales teams are commonplace. I'm supposed to remind everyone of the risks of thoughtlessness in marketing ethical drug products. I've been trying to stop some behaviors for months, with zero results but increasing irritation from the sales leadership. Bad behaviors are expected in any launch with new people. It's the leadership reaction I can't understand."

"Tell me what they're doing. Be precise."

"You seriously want to hear it?"

"Am I your relative, a law enforcement officer, or are you engaging me as an attorney? I can practice in Florida." Fox continues to play on his phone. "The hesitation you exhibit reflects a much larger picture. Spit it out, Cousin."

Alvie moans. "I need bourbon, then. You want one?" She waves at Grace, who's at work in the kitchen area of the large, open room. "Gracie! Come over here and listen, too. You're the bioethicist. Hark, bioethical missiles, incoming!"

"Tell Fox about the threatening behavior, cousin." Grace sits on a large leather footstool.

"I'm overreacting."

"You're not," Fox mumbles. "Bring me a drink."

Alvie carries a bottle of Blanton's bourbon over and sprawls into the leather chair, shoving her size ten feet onto Gracie's stool. "Move over, tiny woman. I need to stretch to breathe. Here's the fact set. Phaelon launched two new drugs. A problem with pricing popped. We pulled a formulation of a new product from the market soon after launch. Irritating but not fatal."

"Extremely irritating to leadership and Wall Street, I'd offer." He pours two drinks. "You want wine, Gracie-girl?"

"My wine is on the kitchen counter. I lubricate my creative culinary talents *en place*."

"Continue the set-up, cousin."

"The sales are nowhere near targets," Alvie says. "I got a call from one of our accountants. Her name is Eddie, short for 'Edna.' Super upset. The Sales Director for the failing product came to her office, bullying her. Demanded she move units to 'recognized sales' inappropriately, to increase quarterly numbers. He told her she was at fault for the team missing their target. Eddie was in tears. I convinced her to go see George, the HR attorney, with me. Stupidly, I said he would help her. Shove the sales guy off her back."

"*Sarbanes-Oxley* implications. This story's sinking fast. But despite the reporting and warnings you gave, you got no help." Fox mutters, head in his game.

"No. In fact, George was skittery and told me Eddie was 'fragile.' Said she was reading the sales guy wrong. He warned me away from her; went on about her being a troublemaker. I pushed back hard. The 'fragile troublemaker' nonsense offended me." Alvie frowns. "And I'm famously difficult to offend."

Fox raises his head to peer at the ceiling. "No chance she misinterpreted the brand director's statements? Could he be whinging out the stress of his own sales failure?"

"No chance. It's not the first time he's come into her office. Eddie is the best we have in accounting." Alvie squirms in her chair, drinking the bourbon. "This comes on the back of separate reports from two National Account Managers telling me about sales misusing sample programs. Those National Account people usually stay in their lanes, so it got my attention."

"*Sarbanes-Oxley, False Claims Act*, possible violations of multiple civil and criminal statutes. I could go on. Orange jumper time."

Alvie sighs. "Not without additional and more serious violations. Minor, non-malicious misuse of programs isn't unusual. Right now, it may be nothing more than a few instances of inadvertent miscommunication. My work is to fix behavior before it becomes a violation. Literally my written job description and how I'm evaluated. It's what I do."

"Here's what I do, Alvie. I evaluate the patterns across behaviors and add in the stressed conditions as a variable. You're describing a significant, worrying pattern. Don't you advise the CEO and the Compliance Committee on matters affecting Security and Exchange Commission risks?"

"Arrggh, Ellis, yes, but I try to fix issues way lower than C-suite level when I can. The thing is, when I questioned the failing product's brand VP, Patrick, he reacted with hostility. Within minutes, my boss, Mike, called me. Mike said Patrick told him to 'get your c-word in line.' Except he didn't say 'c-word.' Then, weeks later, in Vegas, the unofficial official warning."

"Well, you have a problem, Alvie." Fox stops playing his game and stares at his dark screen. "Why are you acting as though you don't?"

"I'm doing my actual job. I've been doing this for years. These aren't issues I would describe as 'panic ready' yet. I'm well-respected. I want to give it time to level out. Damn, they gave me a national award for my work at the Vegas meeting and asked me to move here, to Boca full-time. So confusing. None of this is clear to me."

"This confusion—the lack of clarity—is the screaming alert indicating you face an emergency." Fox finishes his bourbon and puts his phone on a glass side table. "I won my game. Let's figure this out before I need to start another. Here's what you do. Call Penelope Shartrew, at Shartrew and Griffin. Her office is in Dupont Circle. I've texted you her number. Call now."

"Dupont Circle is in DC. Why am I calling a DC attorney?"

"You have an office in DC. You still own your home there,

yes? Nexus, first year of law school? DC is a much better jurisdiction for an employment case. Plus, DC has Penny Shartrew."

"Employment case? They gave me a big-ass national award a month ago. I'm moving down here to work at HQ."

"No 'buts.' Call Penny now. Mention me to her assistant. Remind her you're Grace's cousin. Penny will call you back."

"I think this is an overreaction, Fox. Why am I calling her?"

"You're not overreacting, pet. Just the opposite. You're an attorney. We're trained to under-react to conflict. Never mind, I'll call her office." He pushes off his chair and strides across the room, dialing his phone.

Penelope Shartrew calls Alvie back less than five minutes later. Penny doesn't mention Fox, she just growls, "I need you in my office on Monday, January 2. Bring nothing. 11:30 a.m."

Alvie disconnects from the brief call, shaking her head. "Ok, now, Ellis Argall. Who is Penny Shartrew?"

"Want another?" Fox picks up the bottle of bourbon. "She's a bulldog employment attorney. The best in DC, probably the country."

"Employment. I need someone who understands health law. This is giving me heartburn. It feels like I'm starting a war."

"You're responding to a war someone else has already started. You understand health law. I understand health law. We need Penny, who understands employment law. This is about to get ugly. Your company has decided to go after their *de facto* compliance officer. Think. Think, Alvie. Why would they do such a thing? There's a puzzle."

"Fox, no one's gone after me, not really. Not yet."

"Yes, they have. The termination will occur in a matter of days, Alvie. Days. You're going to be fired any minute for internal whistleblowing. I want you in front of it."

Chapter Three: Now It's Complicated

Fox Argall stands in his library, looking at his phone as it rings. Hesitating, he finally answers. "Penny."

"Ellis. They just pulled the very dead fucking body of Glenn Galileo Heath—yes, that's his damn name—out of the inlet near the Florida Atlantic University. I don't have any details of the suicide. It's in your jurisdiction, right? He's the head of clinical research at Phaelon. I haven't told Alvie yet."

"Good grief, Leona. Suicide? What makes it suicide? How are you sure so soon? Who's Glenn Heath?"

"OK, I'll slow it down for you. Glenn Heath runs Phaelon's clinical research. Think about it. Two patients die. Your drug is yanked from the damn market," Penny sighs. "The second new item is *très* interesting. I'm hearing a Phaelon C-suite exec is about to be indicted."

"Indicted? For what?"

Penny giggles, and it sounds like a track for a horror movie. "Insider trading."

"Insider trading? That's insane."

"Ralph Morton is their lead counsel. The asshole. I mean, what the hell? Like no one was going to notice his stock sales on the heels of two patient deaths?"

"Pen, your 'I don't think much of humans' side is showing."

"You're one to talk, Dr. Argall."

"I've a legitimate diagnosis to explain my gaps in social awareness. You do not."

"Yeah, well, I have twenty damn years of seeing assholes every day. The torture has created my neurodiversity. I'm damaged."

"I'm pretty sure that's offensive, as is your incessant use of vulgar language. It's pathologic. Leaving your personality aside, let me summarize. The head of Phaelon's clinical team —Glenn Heath—was found dead in suspicious circumstances. Ralph Morton, their lead counsel, is about to be indicted. Your theory of the case is that the executives are in fatalistic tailspins."

"Exactly," Penny snorts. "Someone should put the top lawyer on suicide watch."

"Pen. Good grief," Fox mumbles. "You call Heath's death a suicide. I'm a criminal investigator, and such a leap at an early stage makes me squirmy."

"Squirmy." Penny moves away from the phone and says, "He's squirmy about the Heath incident being suicide."

"Who you talking to, Pen?"

"I'm making derisive faces about your use of 'squirmy.' Is that a science word?"

"Can we just say the man is deceased at this point? We've another problem. The death will surely hit the news headlines today. We need Alvie in the loop before she finds out from someone else. Will you call her or shall I?"

"If I call her, I would bill her," Penny laughs. "You call her. Listen, Ellis. Heads up. I'm betting I receive a summons from Phaelon today. It might be tomorrow, but it'll be soon. When I do, I'll be formally asking you to join my team on the Florida side. I need a health care attorney who's not my defendant."

"A wild current flows underneath this situation, Pen. It's not at all clear what's creating the chaos."

"'A wild current.' Settle down, your Welsh poetic pessimism is leaking out. It's the normal idiot company full of people acting like idiots. Over in a blink."

"If only you were correct, pet. If only I was wrong, but I'm not. This will be quite a strain on my cousin. And my wife." He runs his finger on a picture of a college-aged Grace that sits on his desk.

"And here comes the famous Ellis Argall *pathologic* devotion to his Gracie," Penny snarks. "We all have our personality crutches, don't we, Doctor? Focus. They hired a lawyer out of Florida. If they file in your state, I need you."

"I understand."

"Chill, my old friend. Let me do my thing. When I sink my teeth in I'm hard to beat; it's why you love me. I'll call when the complaint lands in my hands. Can you get the time off your detective side hustle?"

"I told my captain some time ago I'd need a sabbatical. It was clear where this was going at Thanksgiving."

"Sabbatical?" Penny guffaws. "You're an odd dude, Ellis."

The connection goes dead.

A loud banging starts outside the window, and Fox drags himself out of his chair to stare at the alley. *Did I put out the trash?*

"Lad! Did you put out the trash?" Grace calls from the kitchen. "Your turn, can't blame me."

"Yes, pet." He taps his head on the wooden shades. *Alvie's right. Nothing makes sense. Pieces are missing. How does the dead researcher fit in? The insider trading? Are they connected?* He dials his cousin. "Alvie, I have some troubling news."

"Glenn Heath is dead." Alvie's voice is flat. "They're saying suicide, but I'm telling you the man would never commit suicide. He had the healthiest ego I've ever run into."

"So, you suspect something more criminal or an accident?"

"I don't know, Ellis. It's all crazy. I keep using the word, but it's truly insane. No reason for this fight, yet they're on the attack."

"Alvie, you're a smart lawyer. If you say it makes little sense, that's enough for me. Let it play out a bit more. Try to think of it as a puzzle we're putting together, with Penny's help."

"I'm trying. It's difficult."

"Sit, calm yourself, and write everything you remember. Categorize it all. Sticky tab everything, color-coded. Make my obsessive heart proud. That's how you spend your time now. Do you want Gracie to stay with you?"

"What? Take your Gracie away? I want you in high spirits. You keep your girl close by your side. Marley still needs her mother. How is your girl doing without Josh? How is her internship going?"

Marley announced to me at Thanksgiving she's quitting medicine. Fox doesn't say it out loud. "Um... well, I guess fine. She's fine. Normal."

"Our Marley's anything but normal. I guess it's par for the Argall course."

"Ah. Well. I understand your point. She appears normal to me."

Fox's voice trails off, the Brick Breaker tune chittering.

"We'll talk later, cousin. Tell Gracie to call me if she wants. This not working is killing me. Too much time on my hands."

"No, you don't have too much free time. You have a new full-time job. Pull your notes together, Alvie. Phaelon will refuse to turn over every document for as long as possible. I'll require your memory of a document to demand it. Your new job starts now."

Two hours later, Penny calls Alvie. "Alvie, we have some news. Ellis is also on the line. We received notice of a complaint.

They intend to file in Florida, so I'm recommending Ellis as our counsel there. You must approve this."

"I figured we'd need Florida counsel." Alvie's voice fades. "Ellis, you want this? Is Captain Harley signed off on you larking about?"

"Let me worry about Cap. I'm their only MD/PhD/JD, and they generally give me my head."

"What other choice do they have?" Penny cackles. "Like you're remotely fucking controllable."

"Pen," Fox sulks. "I'm saddened by this criticism. I'm quite collegial with my team here. They seem to like me."

"I thank my stars you landed in Florida, Ellis, and not DC. I didn't relish a decision about recruiting you."

"Not sure this is a compliment."

"I'll clear that right up," Penny snarls. "Coming from me, it's a huge fucking compliment."

Made in the USA
Las Vegas, NV
03 September 2023

76991310R00122